The Singing Hill

by

Deryn Stewart

Grosvenor House
Publishing Limited

The right of Deryn Stewart to be identified as the author of this
work has been asserted in accordance with Section 78
of the Copyright, Designs and Patents Act 1988

This book is published by
Grosvenor House Publishing Ltd
Link House
140 The Broadway, Tolworth, Surrey, KT6 7HT.
www.grosvenorhousepublishing.co.uk

This book is a work of fiction. Any resemblance to
people or events, past or present, is purely coincidental.

A CIP record for this book
is available from the British Library

ISBN 978-1-83975-026-7

*To my father John Chudley, author of 'Candle-lit Quest',
for all his support and encouragement.*

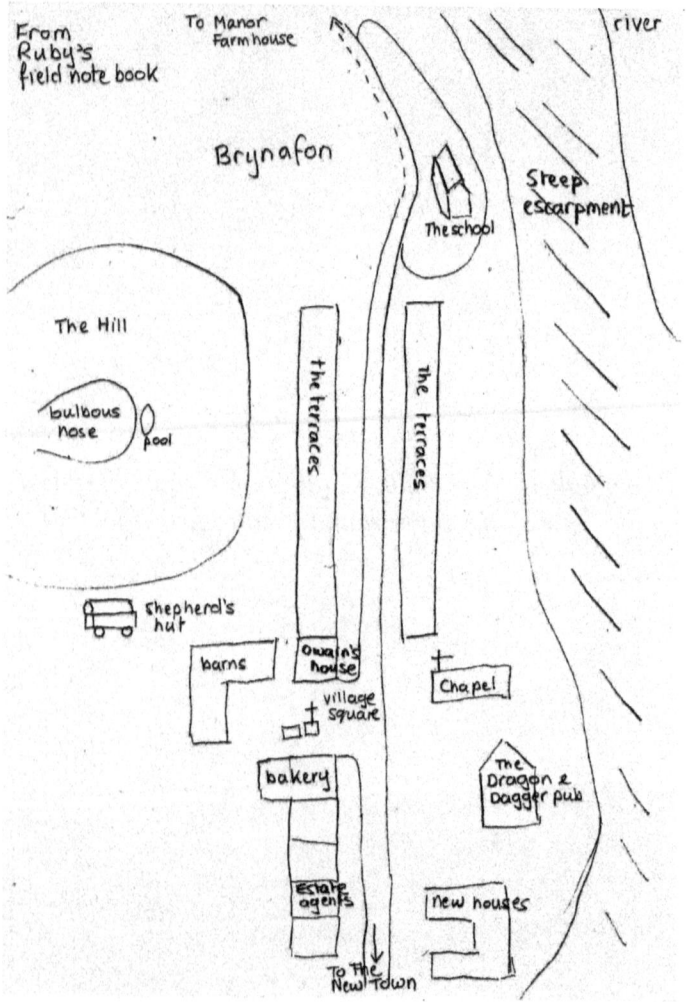

From Ruby's field note book

To Manor Farmhouse

river

Brynafon

The school

Steep escarpment

The Hill

bulbous nose

pool

the terraces

the terraces

shepherd's hut

barns

Owain's house

Chapel

village square

bakery

The Dragon & Dagger pub

Estate agents

new houses

To The New Town

Chapter 1

He was struggling, his arms flailing wildly, his legs
kicking at his captor as he was lifted bodily off his feet,
his arms pummelled the man's chest. He was desperate,
past caring, he fought back with every ounce of energy
in him.

"No, no, nooooooo!"

He tried to twist and turn and bite the arm that held
him, but it was no use. He was in the air, suspended
above the ground, legs swinging. Strong, squat muscular
arms held him tightly. He was being bodily carried off
the hillside. The rain stung at his face, and the wind tore
at his hair. He was shivering violently and in the early
stages of hypothermia.

"No, no, nooooooo!"

His scuffed brown school shoes kicked repeatedly at
his captor's shins, but the small squat man carrying him
hardly seemed to notice. The boy reached up to try and
scratch the bristled face, but the head expertly turned
away from him. The man held him firm, as he carried
the boy, still yelling loudly across the road. The man
opened the tatty, paint peeling wooden door of one of
the terrace cottages that lined the street, expertly
holding the struggling boy in one firm arm.

"I've got him!"

The boy was suddenly thrust forward, his body bumping violently against the brown wooden kick panels below the stairs.

With a start Evan woke up, sweat pouring off him, shaking, just as he had many times before over the past twenty years.

It was always the same. He was on The Hill, that slight rise that rose like a bulbous nose behind the cottages on the west side of the street. He was six years old, in his school uniform with his scuffed, slightly small brown school shoes. He hadn't come home for tea. He'd been up on The Hill, where he always was, just sitting and being, rocking slightly in tune with the invisible waves of The Hill. It was dark, raining and windy. His school blazer was soaked through, his leather satchel sodden. It was past his bed time. He didn't care he was cold, hungry and wet, he was where he wanted to be – on The Hill.

Then his father had come and forcibly carried the protesting Evan back to his home, a small terraced house on the other side of the street.

It had been the same since he was four years old until his father could physically not pick him up and carry him back any more.

Evan strode to the window and stared out into the street, there was not much to see. A row of Victorian terrace houses, identical to the row he was in, ran north, south along a narrow embankment either side of the road. Further up the road at the end of the terraces where he had lived was the Victorian primary school, St Peter's, that had been his childhood school for the first six years of his school life. He had been happiest out in the playground, a long thin strip of asphalt that hugged the terrace below the school, wedged in the confines between the road and the steep sloping valley side that dropped to the river. He had been decent enough at football, rugby and cricket to always be picked for the school teams, sport had been his favourite subject at school, followed surprisingly by history. He couldn't see it from the window but further up the valley was the Victorian farm house that had owned the land all around and the village, and who's philanthropic Victorian owner, one George Sinclair, had built the cottages on the both side of the road, the school and the chapel for the estate workers. The cottages and land had mainly been sold off piecemeal when his son, Henry, had squandered most of the family's wealth on a gambling habit.

Looking out in the other direction he could see the chapel on the same side of the road as the school, but at the opposite end of the village. It was a small low building, unassuming, set slightly back from the road, with the bus stop convenient placed outside it for chapel goers. Evan was not one of them, he'd been escaping his mother at chapel since the age of four to play on The Hill. He knew his mother had suffered the taunts of "that godless son of yours that worships at The Hill." He chuckled to himself, in a way he supposed it was true, he'd always preferred to be at The Hill than chapel, although his mother still faithfully went every Sunday and seemed content to still do so. He did, however, frequent the village pub, the Dragon and Dagger, another slightly later Victorian building that, much to the pastor's disgust was sited right next to the chapel, again set slightly back and on a slight rise at that point. Evan could vaguely remember impassioned sermons on the demon drink issuing from the pastor's lips, with his arms flailing wildly, and what little was left of his hair standing on end, best of all the pastor's face would go bright red, and Evan had expected him to explode like a firework at any moment. As a child Evan had thought it was the most entertaining part of the service by far. Strangely, Evan, unlike his friends did not drink alcohol, the whole experience of alcohol he found after one or two binges in his youth left him unimpressed, and he far preferred the taste of coke or orange juice anyway, so he left it at that. Like the taunts about The Hill, the taunts about his lack of alcoholic consumption had stopped years ago. A sober Evan, with a rather good right hook was no match for his drunken assailants. Evan smiled to himself, perhaps some of the old pastor's words had sunk in somehow and done some good, who knows? He certainly did not fritter his money away on booze like some of his friends, he had better things to keep it for. He had a goal.

Opposite from the old bakery end of terrace house he was now residing in was what was left of the market square, with its war memorial, stone horse trough, working water pump and cobbled courtyard with the dilapidated farm buildings of Owain on two sides of the square with its rusty metal gate where the cows and sheep used to be driven out of down the road to market in The New Town. Further down on this side were a few more shops, a post office and general store and the estate agency. The New Town was a good forty minutes' drive down the valley, but the road was fairly straight as it hugged the terrace cut out of the side of the valley, before it gradually descended to the flat valley floor of the New Town with its railway. In his youth Evan had thought the New Town was the centre of everything that glittered and shone, as he only ever visited once a year with his Mum just before Christmas, when he also went to the dentist, which was not so good.

Looking out of the window to the house opposite that had been his childhood home. Evan brushed the beaded sweat left over from his nightmare from his forehead, and wandered over to get himself a fresh white T-shirt. He glanced back at the dark tousled head on the bed behind him, her white flesh looked even whiter, with a pearly luminescence in the moonlight coming in from the window where he had moved the curtain back. She slept peacefully, he hadn't disturbed her, that was good. Things were better now he was in his twenties, so much better.

Evan had been four years old when he had first discovered The Hill. He remembered the event vividly. He had been shopping with his mother, and they were walking back to their cottage just up the street. His mother had stopped to talk to a neighbour across the road at number 35, when he heard or rather felt its call. He glanced around, not sure where the feeling was coming from, not sure what drew him on. His mother was well in flow now to Hilda at number 35 about the horrendous price of lamb at the butcher's, so she didn't notice when Evan twisted from her grasp and dashed to the west side of the street. He looked at all the houses intently, trying to feel what was calling him onward, where was it coming from? He screwed up his eyes and stared at the terrace cottages, no, it was not one of those calling him. He shook his head, the call or song seemed to be coming from behind the terraces, there was a westerly wind blowing quite strongly that day, it blew his cap over his eyes, Evan took the cap off, holding it in his small hand. He looked along the row of terraces and to the last terraced house at the top end of the road. He saw it was easy to get up the side of the last house across a bit of wasteland. At the end of the garden there was a hole in the hedge, low down and small, as if a fox might frequent it, which he later learnt it regularly did. He lay on his tummy, leaving his satchel on the ground, and wiggled his way head first through the hole. Standing up he realised he had not come out in the back garden of the end terrace house, but had come out diagonally on to the field behind, just after the barbed wire fencing that encircled The Hill. He stood up and stared.

The Hill rose to the height of the cottage roofs. It was the shape of a Welsh rugby ball, with that curious bulbous like nose in the centre. Sheep stared back at him, a hardy native hefted breed. They came on to The Hill at lambing time, and Evan could see the many lambs prancing by their mothers, running, playing, eating, suckling. He smiled, he was home. There wasn't much else on The Hill, an old rotting shepherd's hut was part way up The Hill on the far side, surrounded by stinging nettles, and there was a water trough fed by a tributary off a small stream.

Over the years, every day sunshine, rain or snow Evan visited The Hill. He'd play endless games of dragons and crusaders with his school friend Pete on The Hill, he had his first kiss with Sian age 12 on The Hill.

The Hill was owned by Owain the local sheep farmer, it was more of a small holding than a farm. Owain lived at the other end of the terrace cottages, in a slightly bigger cottage with a small barn attached at right angles, he owned The Hill behind the row of cottages and had grazing rights to the moorland and hills beyond. He owned a small flock of native breed sheep, and to Evan he seemed as old as the hills themselves, even then. He also seemed perpetually grumpy, and having a small boy playing night and day on his land didn't help. Evan's parents were used to an outraged Owain swearing in Welsh and worse for drink banging on their front door with his staff.

"That blasted loony boy of yours is in my field again!"

The local policeman had even been called, but on the third time gave up. Evan was a child, he wasn't hurting the sheep, the sheep even seemed to like him and nudged up to him for titbits and strokes, often knocking the small boy off his feet. Evan could often be found in the evenings, curled up between the sheep in a scrape in the hillside, sleeping peacefully.

That was about the only remarkable thing in Evan's life. He smiled to himself, he must have been a bit of a nightmare for his parent's really, although his mother fortunately seemed to love him whatever.

His school report said with variance "Doesn't really seem to see the point of school." He was averagely intelligent, fairly sporty, his grades read an average C. He was well liked by both pupils and staff, and he had a quiet, assured disposition, a friendly open face, he was polite, helpful when asked, rarely did or handed in any homework, and was not considered to have sufficient calibre or motivation to go to University. He was not seen of sufficient sporting calibre to try out for the Welsh junior rugby squad. The only blot on his copy book was when Gareth the local primary school bully had teased him three days running about his love of the Hill. Evan had always been a placid child, but not this time, his friend Pete saw the sparking fire in his eye, and with a sudden right hook that would have done any Welsh boxer proud, Gareth suddenly found himself ignominiously flat on the school playground. Evan could have sworn the earth shook as he was slain. Gareth had badly miscalculated as Evan was strong from helping with the sheep, and Gareth was taken completely by surprise, it was the last time he teased or bullied Evan about the Hill. Both boys were suspended for two days. Evan thought his family took it remarkably well. His mother said Gareth's family had always been trouble and he was to keep away from him, and his father was secretly proud that Evan had shown a bit of character at last. His father had done a fair amount of amateur boxing himself in his youth and was quietly rejoicing at Evan's splendid right hook. (He had made sure he heard the tale directly from Pete's mouth.) Fighting in the playground, which was the school's version of events, he thought scarcely did it justice, there was no fight just a straight knock out!

As it transpired there was really only one thing outstanding about Evan, and that was his fascination with The Hill. The term fixation was bandied about in those days, to be replaced by the word obsession later on. As Evan was otherwise an easy child at school no expert was ever called, or any expert opinion delivered.

The only upset in Evan's life was when his Dad died of a heart attack, brought on by a life of hard labour, when Evan was twelve, but on the whole Evan viewed this as a bonus, it meant he was not taken from The Hill any longer.

His mother, if anything, seemed happier. The smell of drink that was often on her breath increased, and the bottles now stood openly around the living room, and her mother came from up the valley to live with them, and the women drank happily together. Within a few weeks Evan's mother had secured a part time job serving at the local bakery. People were kind to a widow in Evan's village, and his mother seemed happier than she had ever been. Evan mended what was needed, and lifted anything heavy, in fact had his school report listed any practical subjects, which it didn't, it would have had to have said he actually had a knack for woodwork and making and mending. At eleven Evan had gone down the valley with the rest of the children to secondary school, where he stayed until 16 years gaining average grades in seven subjects, despite frequent bouts of absence, spent sometimes studying at The Hill. His mother was proud of his achievements, she had no qualifications and had had to go straight out to work.

Chapter 2

It was on Evan's way home after the final day of his exams, he saw the advertisement in the estate agents for a trainee negotiator. Bill Clackett, the negotiator was worked off his feet that June, there was an unexpected upturn in the housing market in the valley, and that he desperately needed an assistant, preferably someone younger with plenty of energy. Bill Clackett was beginning to feel his fifty-five years. He was impressed immediately when the young man with the open face, easy smile and relaxed manner walked in. The young man was polite and tidy, and offered a hand to shake immediately, he had a nice voice and had a mature manner for one so young. Had Evan's school had a report on any type of social skills, he would have had a good grade in that, but unfortunately it didn't. Evan secured the job immediately.

Two years later Evan found himself senior negotiator in the newly opened Brynafon office in his home village. Evan really was the one and only choice for the job, he knew the village thoroughly, spoke English and Welsh and had a good grasp of estate agency, he engendered trust in his buyers, with his easy relaxed manner, which spoke, "everything will be alright, you'll see, just leave it to me." and they did. Brynafon was changing too, it was now popular with young families who could not afford the high prices in The New Town, terrace houses were being gutted and done up by their young owners, front doors and gates were painted in a rainbow of colours and brightly coloured flowering baskets were appearing.

There was one unusual new arrival though in the village that immediately sparked Evan's interest, and that was Ruby Red.

It was about the time that Evan became manager of the Brynafon branch of the Estate Agents in his own right, with the pay rise that went with it, that Ruby arrived, in what he knew now was her own unmissable way.

He'd been having a celebratory drink to mark his newly appointed managerial post with his mates at the local pub, The Dragon and Dagger, when he first heard talk of her. The words, whore, prostitute and easy goer were banded about quite freely. She'd been nicknamed Ruby Red because of her appearance, after someone had heard her name was Ruby and her bright red lipstick. If Evan had been a drinker, he would have doubted the clarity of what he was hearing, but as he teetotal he knew he had heard accurately.

"You not seen her then, Evan?" Asked Pete his long-time childhood friend, and always first with the girl gossip in the village.

"Nope, too busy working." Commented Evan.

"Skirt up to here," David his mate, indicated to the top of his leg.

"Black tights, holey, black shoes, red, red lipstick, raven black hair to her collar, and white translucent skin like an unblemished boiled egg." Added Mick, he'd always had a way with words and been top of their English class at school.

"Uh huh," commented Evan casually downing his coke. But secretly he was intrigued. Young, unattached female visitors were a rare occurrence in Brynafon, and this particular young female sounded even more unusual. Most could be accounted for as nieces or relatives of the various parishioners, plus the occasional, usually accompanied female walker. But this particular young lady seemed to have no connection to anyone, and had appeared almost magically out of thin air. There was a baited pause while Pete ordered another round for them all.

"Can't miss her," commented Pete, "She's been sleeping at the bus stop opposite your shop for these past few nights. Bloody cold for someone so skinny." Pete was not without feelings. "She arrived on a bus from Bristol it's said....or it could have been Chester."

That night on his way home, Evan made a point of looking out for her, but she wasn't sleeping at the bus stop. Evan was curiously disappointed, but hoped she'd found somewhere warmer to sleep, it seemed a cold miserable place for such an exotic and frail creature to be. It was to be a whole week until he met her, and then it was thanks to his Mum.

Evan had been sleeping rough on the Hill for years on and off and he knew just how cold the nights could be. Since he'd been ten he'd also been working nights on the Hill.

Owain, the farmer, had long since given up complaining about Evan, although he still grumbled a lot. In fact, Evan had become very useful to him, and even if he didn't like to admit, essential. He also quietly found himself looking on Evan as the son he had never had. Owain had never married, he would have liked to have been, had a wife, had a son like everyone else, someone to pass his farm, his life's work, his father's and his grandfather's life work before him on to. His sweet fiancée had tragically been killed in a landslide in heavy rain on her bicycle as she cycled home, one dark winter's night on the road from New Town to Brynafon, nearly on the eve of their marriage. Owain had never inwardly gotten over the loss. It had totally devastated him, left him empty, alone, without hope or a future, it was just him and his sheep now. It was when he had started drinking.

Owain's health had been deteriorating for some time, a hill farmer's life was tough for someone in their seventies, and Owain's penchant for whisky and pipe smoking didn't help. Evan had been helping with lambing since he was eight years old, by ten years old, the tall, strong lad with the broad shoulders was quite adept. Later on, Evan would muse if he really was his father's biological son, as he stood a good foot taller and had sandy blonde hair with grey/blue eyes, unlike the small, dark, stocky Welshman that had raised him.

It was a bitterly cold, a chilling to your bones, north wind blowing straight down Brynafon, rain turning to snow on that Spring night, when the then ten year old Evan and Owain were lambing a sheep with triplets that Owain, gasped, held his chest and collapsed. He lay there motionless, face down in the cold mud and wet snow. Evan delivered the third, yet unborn lamb swiftly himself, turned Owain over, made sure his airways were clear, rubbed his chest, put his school blazer over the unconscious man, and dragged him, half over one shoulder, off The Hill to the farmhouse at the end of the terrace, where an ambulance was called. It even made the local paper and Evan received his first and only ever prize, a book on mediaeval chivalry at school, for services rendered to the community. His Dad even had time off work to come to the awards service. Evan, then age ten, stayed off school for three days and finished the lambing by himself until Owain discharged himself from hospital and staggered back.

That summer Evan borrowed his father's tools without his knowledge, and with much sawing and banging fixed up the old shepherd's hut in a crude manner, so that Owain would at least have somewhere out of the biting wind to lamb from. Evan used some old pallets purloined from the pub, to replace the rotten floor boards and side timbers. He fixed the holes in the roof by using some old corrugated iron sheets that lay around the farm, and were left over from the remains of a pig byre. If Owain noticed at all, he didn't say anything as corrugated iron was shifted noisily from one place to another. He vaguely presumed that Evan and Pete might be making some type of den for their crusaders and dragons game. The shepherd's hut was at least now weatherproof. His mother knitted a blanket out of the local sheep's wool, spun for her by Hilda for the hut, and each year Evan set about on little improvements to the shepherd's hut. A homemade double-glazed window that would actually open, he made a bed (more pallets), two chairs and a fold down table. This year the estate agency had got rid of an old safe, and Evan had ingeniously made it into a wood burner for the hut. His mother had given him a cushion, and that and his mother's wool blanket kept Owain then

Evan warm on cold nights. In fact, it was probably one of his mother's wool blanket that had saved Ruby's life.

People were straight forward and kind in Brynafon. First a woolly handmade Welsh blanket had appeared for Ruby at her bus stop, and a casserole. Followed the next day by a cushion for her head and a flask of hot soup. By the day after there were freshly baked scones and a pot of jam and a hair brush.

The pastor at the local chapel was above all a good man, gruff, stoic and with a strong opinion on everything, and when he heard of a young girl sleeping rough at the bus stop outside his chapel, he immediately did what a good Christian man would in his position, and offered her a bath, a good hot meal, prepared by his wife and a bed on the pew of the chapel, where there was also a little kitchen and basic facilities. He told his congregation in no uncertain terms a job was needed and that good Christian men and women of faith should put their faith into action. One heard the call and responded which was how Ruby Red began work at the local bakery with Evan's mother.

Chapter 3

On his promotion Evan had moved out of his mother's and was now living permanently in the shepherd's hut on The Hill, which suited him perfectly. So, he hadn't seen his mother and didn't know that Ruby now worked in the bakery.

The first thing he noticed was that the bakery looked different. There were two tables with an assortment of chairs outside and two tables inside. There were flowers on the tables, and bright table covers. Young mothers with children were having coffee and chatting and laughing. Ruby had noticed that the growing numbers of young mothers in Brynafon had nowhere to go, and this had been her idea in her first week. It was a roaring success and business had already increased threefold. Later in the month the Chapel opened its first mother and toddler club.

Evan had not had any fresh bread in that morning for his sandwiches, so he called into the bakery before work. Ruby Red was the first thing he saw. She was different to any girl he had ever seen in these parts. Of medium height, she was as his friend said, stick thin, with white alabaster skin. She wore a black, stretchy short skirt, her black tights still had holes in them and her black flat pumps were well worn. Her lips were a vivid ruby red, and her black hair was piled on top of her head. Her eyes were dark ringed with black liner that curled up at the corners, and her Roman nose gave her an exotic air. She had something of an Amy Winehouse look about her, he thought. He stopped as she turned from helping old Mrs Davis with a loaf that was high on the shelf. He had meant to see his mother to be served, but she had a queue. His mother smiled at him as she saw him. Ruby caught the smile, she addressed him directly.

"You're Evan," she said. Her accent wasn't from around the Welsh borders.

"Yes," he said, rather obviously, unusually he was lost for words. His throat felt dry. He had suddenly developed a prickle in his throat and a dry cough.

"Tell me about this Hill of yours then," she said.

Most people teased Evan about his fixation about The Hill. His mates from school were all used to him and his ways, and just took it that was what Evan did, go to The Hill. But people who didn't know him so well, and the teenagers he had met at secondary school teased him about it to his face, and thought he was odd, "bonkers" and "off his rocker" were usually bandied about, and sometimes it was a lot ruder. When Evan had obtained a good job, above the pay grade and prospects of most of his mates, the banter tended to stop. But Ruby was different. She wasn't like the girls who wanted to go out with the odd guy, in a good suit and shiny shoes with a bit of money in his pocket.

She was direct, honest and didn't think it at all odd. She didn't judge him at all, she appeared to accept him for what he was and what he thought. That in itself was a new experience for Evan with girls.

"Tell me about This Hill of yours then," Ruby was saying again to him.

"It's not really my Hill it belongs to Owain Jones the sheep farmer, but I intend to buy it one day." Evan didn't quite know why he was telling Ruby this. He'd never told anyone about his plans before, not even his mother. This was what he had been saving for, for the past few years. There was a queue building up behind them, as Ruby served Evan his bread.

Evan cleared his throat. "Can I buy you a drink and meal at the Dragon and Dagger this evening, and I can tell you about it then?" He enquired. He was half expecting Ruby to say no, for some reason he felt short of breath, his heart was pounding and his hands were sweaty. He hadn't felt like this for any girl before, and not even when he landed the lucrative sale of the manor farmhouse up the valley. He held his breath.....his lungs felt like they were going to explode....would she?.... Wouldn't she?.....

Ruby looked at him with her direct open gaze. "Sure," she said "meet you at 7p.m. then?"

The day just couldn't go fast enough for Evan, it dragged interminably, even though he was fairly busy at work. That evening he had a shower at his Mum's and changed into a clean casual shirt, his newest chinos, and gave his wavy, sandy blonde hair a brush. An open face and with a square chiselled jaw and blue grey eyes looked back at him. He couldn't do anything about his hands which continued to sweat however much he washed them. He decided best not to shake hands with Ruby, just offer her a chair and a drink to start with.

Ruby arrived dead on time, and he ordered her a glass of red wine. He stuck to his usual coke with ice. He could see his mates at the bar were bursting with curiosity at Ruby and not being too delicate about it. There were gesticulations that Evan was about to get lucky and have a very good evening with the local whore. Evan decided it was best to pre-empt the situation, so he briefly introduced Ruby his to his mates at the bar. It was said you could tell a lot of a man's character by his mates, and in this he thought he seemed to have rather dubious taste in some of them. If she was going to walk out on him, surely it would be now, he felt himself holding his breath again, and vowing that now as a responsible adult and senior manager in the local estate agents, he really needed friends to match. Pete was fine of course, and David, well usually. Fortunately, Ruby seemed neither intimidated by them or sought to get know them, she was polite, but gave nothing away and said little, she just sipped her drink demurely and smiled. This he thought was the girl to have by your side in an awkward situation, and he wished the estate agency was doing better so she could work with him, a female estate agent on hand would definitely have its advantages. He would mention it to Bill Clackett.

He steered her deftly to a table as far away from the bar as possible, with a backwards glare at his sniggering mates. Sometimes he wondered if they would ever actually grow up, and this was one of those times he wished they had. Unfortunately, the Dragon and Dagger was not a large pub, and the table remained perilously close to the bar and his friends.

He and Ruby both ordered the Welsh lamb, he wondered if Ruby was as nervous as he was, his knees seemed to be knocking under the table so violently, he thought she would hear them, and he was glad of the napkin to wipe his sweaty hands on. He must be going down with the 'flu' he thought, just his luck. He hoped his face was not red or sweaty. She seemed relaxed enough, her shoulders were down, her arms relaxed in front of her, she looked around the pub curiously, she'd never been in the height of night life of Brynafon before.

"The Dragon and Dagger, that's a funny name for a pub, isn't it? I thought the dragon was slayed by a sword not a dagger," she said.

The name of the Dragon and Dagger had been the inspiration for a lot of Evan's and Pete's childhood games of swords and slaying dragons on The Hill.

"I suppose it is," he said. "I never really thought about it, it fired our imagination for games of dragon slaying on The Hill when Pete and I were kids."

She smiled.

"There was a bronze and gold jewelled dagger found when the pub was constructed in Victorian times. It's in the local museum in The New Town, we went to see it once when I was a kid on a school trip," he said. "It was the best thing about the trip, that and Gareth falling in the river during the picnic in the water meadows." He said with a smile.

The smile was returned.

"This Hill of yours, "she said, "tell me what makes it so special to you."

Evan opened his mouth to speak, then shut it. It had been called "that loony boy's Hill" and quite a few expletives by his late father, but no one had ever asked him before why it was special to him.

He thought, and took another bite of his succulent lamb. It smelt delicious, at least he had not lost his appetite. The food at the Dragon and Dagger could always be relied upon for being, good, wholesome, home cooked fare.

"I'm just drawn there," he said. It sounded weak and feeble saying it like that, and Evan wished he had prepared something better to say about, after all he'd had all day to think about, but strangely all he'd thought about was Ruby's red lips, and dark eyes. There was a pause, Ruby looked thoughtful, her dark eyes with the long lashes and dark eye liner blinked, she looked like she was thinking about her response carefully. Finally, she spoke.

"It feels special....set apart.....sacred, even holy." Said Ruby, it was more of a statement than a question.

He looked up at her, his mouth dropped again. She had just described what he could not, what nobody had until that moment.

"Yes," he said simply, it seemed an inadequate response again.

"The locals always chided my mother that I skipped chapel to worship at The Hill, when I was young." He laughed.

"Hmmm," Ruby seemed to be contemplating and summing up his response with some thought and deliberation, not the usual sneer or laughter he was used to. She twirled her fork around in the gravy for a bit. "Anything else special about it?" She asked. There was not a hint of sarcasm in her voice, just curiosity.

"It sings sometimes," he said. What was he saying? That sounded worse than ever, he was sure she was about to walk out right now, however hungry she was, now she found she was having a meal with the village idiot.

"Sings?" She questioned, again no sarcasm, "describe to me exactly how it sings," she said, putting down her knife and fork and wiping her mouth delicately with her napkin. Ruby definitely seemed, despite her appearance, a bit more cultured than the local girls he thought.

"Yes, it sings, when the wind is coming from the west to the east at a certain angle there is this low, kind of pipe sound, like a low wooden flute," he said. He attempted to approximate the sound, "whooo, ooooo, ooooo."

Ruby laughed, but not maliciously. "Interesting!" She announced.

His mates at the bar heard the laughter, lucky Evan was certainly doing well with this girl. There was a new round of gesticulating arm action to go with it from them.

"Do you think if I had my own Hill I'd be more interesting to the girls?" commented Pete. He had to admit he was just a bit envious of Evan dining Ruby.

"I doubt," it answered David, "you'd do better with a good car to pull them in."

David worked at the local garage. He had a girlfriend, Sian.

"Nothing wrong with my car," announced Pete.

"Apart from the smell, and the fact it doesn't go over 40 mile an hour." Retorted David. They returned to stare at Evan and Ruby, enviously. David just wished he could afford the meal, let alone the girl to go with it, Ruby was a bit special. He concluded that his car and its ongoing maintenance kept him poor.

"Do you think I can see this Hill of yours then?" Ruby was asking.

"You can see it tonight after the meal if you want, it's a good moonlit night, and the bulbous nose on The Hill, is really accentuated in the moonlight."

"Bulbous nose?" Enquired Ruby. He was sure he was sounding worse and worse. Good job he did not drink to add to the effect. He was normally so self-assured, so fluent with his customers, he must be getting the 'flu' quite badly he concluded. He explained about the shape of The Hill.

"Great," said Ruby. The dark eyes and long dark lashes blinked again.

Evan had never had a date go so smoothly, he couldn't quite believe his luck, or why no one else had plucked up the courage to ask Ruby out before, she'd been in town two whole weeks now. She seemed to have a genuine interest in his interest in The Hill. Was she just being polite? It was about as interesting as a stamp collection or steam trains to most people.

Evan in turn asked about Ruby, he was curious to find out more about this exotic creature. Ruby, however, was not letting on a lot about herself. Her name was Ruby Whyte, (not Ruby Red), and as he was later to learn when he sneakily had a look at her passport was Ruby Hetherington-Whyte. She'd been educated in a convent school and was finishing a 3rd year of an archaeology degree when she'd left. She didn't specify why and she did not say where. Her father was in the army and stationed abroad, but Evan didn't get the impression he was an ordinary foot soldier and her mother hadn't liked to travel with him.

One older brother, also in the army and that was it. But Evan had the distinct impression that wasn't it. That was not all there was to Ruby. He just had the distinct feeling, that the uncomplicated girl who appeared to be sitting before him wasn't any of those things. Somehow with that instinct that served him so well in his estate agency business, he knew that Ruby was something else. She was educated, she was bright, analytical, and above all there was a lot else about Ruby that she didn't want to talk about right now. That was OK with him, if she wanted to tell him, if she felt she could trust him, she would, and it made her seem even more beautiful and mysterious and exotic. He definitely wanted to know more about her, and have time to do so. Was she running away from something? Or to something? He did not know. It crossed his mind that he might have some stupid romantic notion about this exotic stranger, but he didn't consider himself romantic or prone to fantasy. His keen observation skills told him something was off, but that Ruby was not intentionally being devious. She was simply dressed in the same clothes she had worn at work that day, only her hair was different, it was newly brushed and let down and hanging to her shoulders. She wore the same black stretchy skirt, the same white blouse, her once shiny black patent pumps were down at the heel, but he knew they were leather and had been good, her black coat was the same, it was 100% wool, he could see the label as it lay over the back of her chair, there was a small discreet gold and red crest on the breast, it wasn't fashionable but functional, it looked like it may have been her old school coat. It was probably what had kept her warm and saved her life that first night sleeping out at the bus stop. She had small, discreet earrings on, gold with a pearl in the centre, their design was classic, and she had one small ring, a ruby with diamonds on her right hand, small, ornate and he thought old, handed down, old money. It wasn't the type of ring a young woman would buy or have bought for her.

There was her manner too, she looked around curiously, she wasn't intimidated by a new place, him or his oaf like friends. She took it all in her stride. Only one thing spoilt the evening, he was getting up to leave, when his friends uninvitedly gathered round.

"Lucky with Ruby Red then, paid for her time then?" Mick emboldened by drink chipped in suddenly and rudely. Pete saw the same fire in Evan's eyes, he'd seen only once before.

"No!" Pete said..... too late.

It was a left hook this time that flattened Mick. Mick had been suddenly dropped from Evan's social circle.

"Her name is Ruby Whyte, not Ruby Red," Evan blurted out, "and she's MY girlfriend." Both he and Mick were promptly served a two week ban by the landlord, which was a shame, because he had wanted to invite Ruby out again next week.

Evan hurried her out quickly, he glanced back to see his friends hanging out of the doorway of the pub, wanting to know if the couple were heading out together. Night life in Brynafon was not up to much.

Evan lead Ruby holding her hand tightly to Owain's farmyard, from where they could access The Hill easily. She shivered slightly in the cold night air.

"We'll just have a quick look, it's a cold out here for you, "he said giving her hand a squeeze. He looked down at her feet with the worn pumps on.

"Do you mind if I carry you?" He asked. "It's pretty muddy through the yard, and stony on The Hill."

She laughed brightly. "Okay."

After carting about sheep, Ruby was easy to pick up and carry, and he quickly made his way deftly up The

Hill until he was half way up, where he put her down gently.

It was a wonderful starry night. There were no street lights to pollute the night sky in Brynafon and little light from the houses.

"Wow," said Ruby looking up. "I'd no idea there could be so many stars!"

"That's the Milky Way," he pointed upwards.

"Wow," she said again. "You don't see this in the city."

Evan was right, the bulbous nose of The Hill was well highlighted in the moonlight and in sharp relief. He thought the moonlight added something to the aura of the place, it seemed more special, more set apart in the quiet of the moonlight. The quiet between them seemed suddenly very special too.

"It's quite something," she said eventually.

Evan was quite relieved, he expected something on the lines of "You dragged me up here, for this!" He was not in the habit of taking girls up here. Sian at 12 years had been the last girl he'd taken here.

"Is it a slag heap, from coal mining?" She enquired.

"No," replied Evan. "Definitely not, there's no mines or coal seams here, it's all down the valley at the New Town. There's never been anything here."

"Hmm," she said mulling it over. "I don't think it's part of the natural."

Evan wasn't sure what "the natural" was.

"What do you mean?" He asked curiously.

"I mean I don't think its natural geology, I think it's more likely to be a manmade structure."

"Oh," said Evan. "I'd never thought of that. It's just The Hill to us."

"There's no history, no legends attached to it locally?" Asked Ruby.

"No nothing that I know of," said Evan. "I can ask Owain, he'd know, but as far as I know it's just a piece of hill that's difficult to farm."

Ruby shivered slightly beside him.

"Do you want to go? It's cold," said Evan. Ruby was not used to being on the hillside like him, fortunately it was an unusually still night.

"No," she said. "Not just yet, I want to get my bearings, so the valley goes down there," she pointed south, "and the river is down there." She pointed east. Wales is west of the river, England east."

"That's right," he said.

"And can you see the river from your Mum's house over the road?" She asked.

"No," he replied, "the trees are too high."

"But if there weren't the trees, and there weren't the two rows of cottages, you'd be able to see the river from where we're standing here?"

"I think so," he said. "I never really thought about it."

"Do you have an ordnance survey map?" She asked.

"No," he replied. "I've never needed one, I've wandered the hills here since I was a child. But there's internet at the estate agency, and I can put one up for you tomorrow evening if you like?"

Ruby did like. This was going much better than he expected.

"Why do you need an ordnance survey map?" He enquired.

"Well, your Hill is on quite a strategic point," she said. "I know it doesn't look like it now, but before there were the cottages I think it may have over looked the river."

Evan took a breath, his Hill had importance! "Wow, you think it may have guarded the river, possibly been a fort or something."

"Possibly" she said, "It probably would have been bigger then, there's bound to have been a lot of erosion with all the rain here over the years and land slippage."

Evan drew in another breath, so he was right, after all these years! The Hill had always felt like something special to him. In its way, it was a terrific relief.

"Did the Romans ever come here?" She asked, "are there any Roman ruins or artefacts found nearby?"

"That old!" Said Evan, he had been thinking more on the lines of mediaeval castles and crusaders. Images of him and Pete play fighting with homemade swords and shields came into his mind. "No, I don't think so, nothing was ever mentioned at school. The Romans were further south, I think like everyone else they just bypassed here!" Everyone except Ruby he thought.

Ruby laughed, "We'll see," she said. "Now show me this shepherd hut of yours, your mother tells me you now call home, I'm getting cold."

So, Evan swung Ruby into his arms and carried her over the threshold into the shepherd's hut, he was not to know at the time what a significant act this was to be.

"It's warm!" Ruby said with relief as soon as he set her down inside.

He had lit the wood burning stove before the meal, and it heated up the small space wonderfully. There was a definite smell of lanolin, it was not unpleasant.

Ruby was rubbing her hands in front of the wood burner and looking at it curiously.

"I made it out of a safe that came out of the estate agency," Evan said, "and I've lined the walls, roof and floor with sheep's wool. It's great insulation, plentiful and cheap in these parts."

"Estate agent, hill sheep farmer and handyman," she laughed. "Quite a combination, a bit more than the average decent looking guy in a suit then!"

Evan smiled. He'd never ever been called anything more than average before, even though his boss did seem to appreciate him fortunately. Bill Clackett had always been good to him. He'd been lucky to have him as a boss he thought.

"It's amazing," Ruby was saying, "Who would think it from the outside, who made the wool rug, and the blanket and curtains, oh, I recognize the rug and cushion – your Mum! I had a similar gift given anonymously to me when I was sleeping at the bus stop, now I know who to thank."

"I've got a lot to thank Mum for," Evan smiled. "The rug is woven on wooden pegs, and the curtains. It's a local craft, some of the older women still do it, and we learnt it at junior school too."

Ruby continued to look around and ask questions with that inquisitive sharp mind of hers.

"So, you've got a couple of paraffin lamps for light then, no electricity?"

"Not quite" said Evan. "I have got a small solar panel on the roof, it gives me a limited amount of electricity, LED lights have really helped the output. It only works in sunny weather for any length of time, so the paraffin lights are a backup."

"What about water, a toilet and a shower?" Asked Ruby ever practical.

"All limited!" He replied. "Water there's plenty of in Wales, that runs off the roof to collect in plastic drums, and I can have that on tap," he slid back a work top."

"One sink, its only cold though, hot water I have to heat on the wood burner. I have a small rather inadequate solar shower, its only warm in the summer. For the rest of the time, I use an old cattle trough outside, when I have to break the ice I go to Mum's still!"

Ruby shivered at the thought.

"Toilet is a compost tip out the back, I add wood shavings and old wool, there is a corrugated iron screen though, I don't like to alarm the odd walker who comes through here in the summer too much!"

Ruby laughed. "Tough guy," she said.

"Remember I've been sleeping and playing on this hill since age four," he said.

Ruby had made herself comfortable on the bed, she had kicked off her shoes, and was swinging her slim legs.

"Have you found anything unusual here?" She asked. As usual Ruby asked the right questions.

"Well actually, yes." Answered Evan. "At least it's just things of interest I've been collecting since a boy." He pulled out an old shoe box, which had a faded picture of a school boys brown lace up shoes on. He took off the lid. He'd never shown these to anyone either.

He held the paraffin light for Ruby so she could clearly see his boyhood treasures. She carefully picked them up one at a time, rolling them over with her hands, and running her fingers over them.

"This," she said. "Is a Neolithic or you would call it, stone age axe head. You've got a good eye for detail; how did you know to pick it up and keep it?"

"It was different to all the stones around it," he said. "It was covered in mud of course, I used my toothbrush to clean it off. Then I could see the little chips in it, and the regular shape. Does it mean anything?" He asked curiously.

"It means people were here for a long time, probably there were more trees then and not so many sheep, the landscape looked different then. Is there anywhere you particularly find the items?" She asked.

"Mainly at the bottom of The Hill, after it rains," he said.

"That makes sense."

"But there's a place half way up, a bit of a dip where water gathers, near where we were tonight that about half of it has come from."

Ruby looked in the box again. There was a broken rod or pin that was weathered green.

"That's bronze," she said, "and this" it was a semi-circular piece of metal about the size of a £2 coin. There was also a squashed bit of metal, again bronze. The final piece was wrapped in old yellowing tissue paper, she carefully opened it.

Even in the dull light she could see a slight shine to the item, and it was surprisingly heavy. It was circular, the size of a couple of £2 pieces, like a large coin, but had holes and a twisted intricate design, it looked like something had once attached to the back of it.

"Wow," she said. "Do you know what this is?" She asked.

"I suspected it was gold, so I took it to the jeweller in the New Town to be valued, it was gold, he said it was old, offered me a tidy sum for it, but it belongs to Owain and more over The Hill."

She nodded. "I think in the morning, you should photograph this. I know someone who could tell you more."

He nodded.

There was a sudden knock on the door.

"Owain" said Evan, Ruby had jumped a mile.

Owain poked his weathered face in. "Didn't realise you'd got company lad," he said in Welsh. He nodded at Ruby. "She's having trouble, think its triplets again."

Evan translated "Sheep trouble," to Ruby.

"I'm coming," he said. "Sorry, I'll be back Ruby, you can see me out of the window." She nodded.

When Evan came back Ruby was in the homemade bed, but she wasn't asleep. Evan, as his mates would have said, had "got lucky." He also had a full time live-in girlfriend. He was lucky indeed.

The next day Evan awoke early. There were sheep and lambs needing attention, their baaing filled the air in the little shepherd's hut. He couldn't sleep anyway, he had too many questions to ask Ruby. He opened the window, a fraction, to get out the fug. A mist blew in. Yes, he had a lot of questions, and he didn't want to pry, but they needed answers, some he already had, and he knew that Ruby was in trouble. He glanced at her small, black clutch bag which was open on the side. Peeking in he saw a black coomb, a tissue, her red lipstick, a black eyeliner, a tampon, a pair of panties, and a passport and driving licence. So, Ruby could drive. Gingerly he pulled out the passport, he hated being sneaky, it wasn't in his nature, quickly, and with a guilty backward glance at the sleeping Ruby. He quickly looked inside it, the face of Ruby Hetherington-Whyte stared unblinkingly out at him.

Date of birth made her 20 years, yes that all fitted. So, she was Ruby Hetherington-Whyte, and she was definitely in trouble, and that was it. That was all she had in the world when she came to Brynafon. No mobile phone, no keys, no wallet, just £70 in notes which, he knew where her wages for the week at the bakery. She had literally left in the clothes she stood in and with her hand bag. From that he could tell, Ruby was practical, well organised, and in a hell of a hurry to get away.

He had seen the fading, now yellow large ugly bruises on the top of her arms, and the on her left thigh. Someone had tried to rape her. He didn't think they had succeeded as she was not sore when he penetrated her, and she had no fear or reluctance with him. He grinned to himself, quite the opposite. But someone had tried to rape her, violent boyfriend? That was the most likely explanation. But why escape and go all the way to Brynafon? Sleep in the cold for three nights, hungry and afraid. Surely, she could have called the police, her mother? Ruby was a practical and articulate young woman. She also had the wounds to prove her ordeal. But above all what worried him, was, was she safe? Was she in danger even now? He was pretty sure she would have not gone to these extraordinary lengths if it had not been necessary, necessary for her very survival. There was another thing that worried him. It niggled in his mind and sat there. Ruby, apart from the physical signs, showed no mental signs of her ordeal. He was used, as an estate agent to see people under mental pressure and duress. He had had to lay a comforting arm upon many. People who had to sell because of bereavement, divorce or being left, people who could no longer afford their mortgages, or who had lost their jobs.

He remembered Tom at school, known by the other children as "tatty Tom" because of his tatty clothes and unwashed face and pungent smell. Tom was always happy at school, he came early, left as late as he could, and was always there, even when he was ill. Tom had bruises and frequent broken bones. His parents never came to parents' evenings. Tom used to shake at home times. He shook even more approaching school holidays. One day, the teacher took Tom to see the Headmaster. A smart lady with a case came for Tom. Tom never went home, or came to school at Brynafon again.

OK Ruby wasn't six years old, but she was not immune either. Whatever had happened was a frequent occurrence, she had become used to it, learnt to deal with it, but this time, perhaps this time was worse, or perhaps she had just had enough, just flipped and run. He didn't know, but he was going to ask. Because he knew from that first evening, he wanted to be the one to keep Ruby safe, to have her by his side for ever. Just like he wanted to be on The Hill for ever.

He quietly put more wood on the stove and blew it back into life. He pulled on his old warm wool sweater, and quietly went outside to tend to the sheep.

When he came back inside Ruby was up, she had the quilt draped round her, and she had managed to put the kettle on the hot top of the stove, she was looking at the pan, and had found the porridge.

Evan laughed, and gave her a big kiss.

"I'll do it," he said. "I'll show you how all the refinements of this place work this evening. But first I have some questions." He said.

"I thought you might," she said, she didn't seem taken back. He ladled out the hot porridge into a bowl for her, fortunately he had two bowls from when Owain stayed.

Thus, it all came out, Ruby was matter of fact and to the point.

She had been studying for a degree in Archaeology, in her third year at Bristol University, and living in halls, when her father had come calling. The first she had known about it, was when her locked door of her room was opened, and he marched in. There were no pleasantries, he made straight for her, pinning her to her bed. Ruby had screamed loudly, before the rough strong had was clapped over her mouth.

"Fortunately, my neighbour Camilla, likes to entertain the rugby team, she's working her way through them, often several at a time," Ruby explained with a smile. "Well, the rugby team like a challenge and a bit of a fight, so hearing my scream, the walls are very thin, several charged into my room, a couple were stark naked, the others following were only in their boxers. They waded in enthusiastically."

Visions of the naked rugby team swarming in the room came vividly to Evan's mind, it was not a pretty sight.

"A good team then?" enquired Evan, it seemed only polite.

"Oh yes," replied Ruby "top Varsity team three years running. Also," said Ruby, "I happened to have in my hand a stone age flint hand axe, which my archaeology professor, had kindly lent me to study. It was still as amazingly sharp as the day it was made, and it yielded quite a cut and blow to his head. I jumped on to the bed, grabbing my coat which I hadn't hung up and my bag, holding it in front of me, and with the axe smashed the window and leapt through it."

"Good God!" Evan was quite appalled.

"I could hear the fight behind me and groans and yells, I plunged out into the bushes, fortunately my room is sunken on the ground floor. I know the site like the back of my hand, as I often jog around it. I went through the bushes for about half a mile, then picked up the road, I just ran flat out to the train and bus stations, the first bus I saw leaving was to Abergavenny, I changed buses there to New Town, again the bus to Brynafon was just pulling out. I had just enough money for the fare. I think the driver let me off some."

"What happened to your Dad?" Asked Evan worried for Ruby's welfare.

"He just kept coming like I knew he would. He was out of the window despite the head injury shortly after me, but he's bigger than me, so the bushes held him up a lot, I could hear him snorting and bashing away. But I gained distance by the time I came to road, I took my shoes off and ran as fast as I could. I was all in black clothing and it wasn't far to the bus station. He didn't have a car or motor bike parked there, my guess it was at the main entrance, he would have had to go back for it."

"This isn't the first time, is it?" Asked Evan.

"You're very perceptive," said Ruby, eyebrows raised.

"No, it's not. When I was at boarding school, he would come and try and get me. In the holidays, I would sometime run away from home back to school." Ruby smiled.

"I remember at my convent boarding school my friends hanging out the upstairs window, I'd be peeking, keeping hidden. Sister Bernadette would be out on the front lawn, all five feet of her, seventy years old and as hard as nails, giving him hell. "Over my dead body, you evil man," she would be saying, and she meant it too. She would not budge, and Sister Regina behind with a rolling pin and apron on, she'd been bread making, and Sister Agnes with a pitch fork, poised ready for action. Sister Agnes is a large Amazonian female, could have easily passed for a man, she was amazing with a spade and fork in the garden, we always though if she hadn't been a nun she would have batted for the other side! They were amazing women. They kept me safe at all cost. They never showed any sign of fear or considered backing down. He tried several times. But that convent was locked up good and proper at nights. He's been posted abroad somewhere in the Middle East for a few years since I've been at University so I wasn't expecting the attack, I didn't know he was back. Thank God I had my passport and driver's licence in my handbag, as I had just opened a new bank account that day."

"What about your Mum, doesn't she know, doesn't she do anything?"

Asked Evan amazed.

"Mum is frigid, she is in her own little world. She doesn't want to know. He doesn't bother with her, he only likes young girls."

Evan was horrified.

"Can't the police do anything?" He asked, already knowing the answer.

"No, he's military intelligence, clearance up to here," Ruby said indicating with her hand a sign as high as her head. "Making things, paper work, computer files and people disappear is what he does for a living. He has no qualms about hurting or killing people, it's his job. He's very good at it."

Evan shivered. How could he keep Ruby safe from a man like that? It was completely above his league, totally, but he was going to do his damnedest to try. He just sat holding Ruby's hand for a while in silence. Letting the enormity of what he had just heard sink in. He believed her alright. It all fitted in, she had not flinched when she told him. He could see the light of the warm memory of the nuns in her eyes, and feel the weight and sharpness of the flint axe in her hand. It was all frighteningly true, he was sure of it. They sipped the warm tea still in silence.

"I'm going to keep you safe." Said Evan, he sounded more confident than he was. He squeezed Ruby's hand tightly. "Well, if you wanted a forgotten back water to hide away in, you couldn't have come to a better place than Brynafon!"

They both laughed.

"How about going back to bed for a bit?" He said with a cheeky smile. Ruby wound her arms playfully round his neck, and pulled him down on to the bed for an answer.

Saturday was busy at work both for Evan and Ruby. She called in at the Estate Agency after her work finished at four. She found Evan busy taking boxes of paper out of a cupboard next to the toilet cubicle, and small kitchen area.

"Give me a hand, will you?" He asked. "I've got big plans for this cupboard." She obligingly held out her arms as Evan loaded her with dusty boxes full of old property details and paperwork. She coughed at the dust. "Through there!" He nodded to the open back door, where Ruby saw a fire burning in the courtyard, already consuming burning boxes in its heart. She threw the boxes on the fire.

"This," he said, turning to the now empty cupboard. "Is going to be our new shower. The estate agency doesn't need the storage space now we're computerised, and it is right next to the sink, so the pipe work should be easy. On Monday, we'll take a trip to the New Town, pick up the bits I need to do it, and you can see the dagger in the museum, and I'll buy you some warm clothes and lunch, sound good?" he enquired.

"Great," she said. "But won't Bill Clackett mind you turning the cupboard into a shower?"

"I hope not, I can get very dirty with this job!" He looked down at his dust covered clothes, they both laughed.

"You know it's a pity you can't finish your degree, you've only got a few months to go. You're not like me, I was no good at school, but you, you're dead sharp." He looked at her. "Is there no one who can help?" He asked.

"I was thinking that too," she said thoughtfully. "There just might be someone... may I use your computer here. I'll need to use your email account."

"Help yourself" he said.

Ruby typed away furiously for five minutes. Another five minutes and an answer came back. It was written to Precious from and C.S Forester. Evan glanced at it, he raised an eyebrow at the Precious.

"It's not what you think," Ruby laughed holding his hand. "It's code, Precious for Ruby, Precious jewel, see, and C.S.Forester is the author of the Hornblower books my Professor's favourite read.

SHE is actually Dr. Elizabeth Mary Forster. She's going to sort it for me to take the exam, and is going to try to get some of my things, and notes for me," Ruby frowned and thought, "Where can I send a box to? It can't be here."

"Send it to Bill Clackett, I'll let him know it's coming, delivery men don't like to get up here, so most things go to the Bill's main office in the New Town, and I pick them up."

There was more typing.

"Job done!" Said Ruby.

On Sunday Evan decided to show Ruby the lie of the land. She was interested in the landscape and how the river related to the village and The Hill. So, borrowing his Mum's wellies for Ruby they carefully made their way down a steep and zigzagging track that lead from the village down to the river. It was softly raining, that fine Welsh soft mist of a rain, and it was hellishly slippery. The wet rocks glistened, and the trees glinted with rain drops. The drops hung like small silver Christmas tree baubles on the end of the pines and larch branches, dropping down their necks as they passed. A squirrel leapt overhead showering them further with wet drops from the trees. Every so often there was a sharp cry of a heron from the river. They could hear the river rushing, getting louder and louder now they came near the end of the path. At some points, they had to climb down backwards over steep sections, and hang on to branches to steady themselves. In places, a scree of mud and stones had obliterated the path, and extreme care was needed to traverse it, at a couple of places a small stream and little waterfall bounced over the stony path.

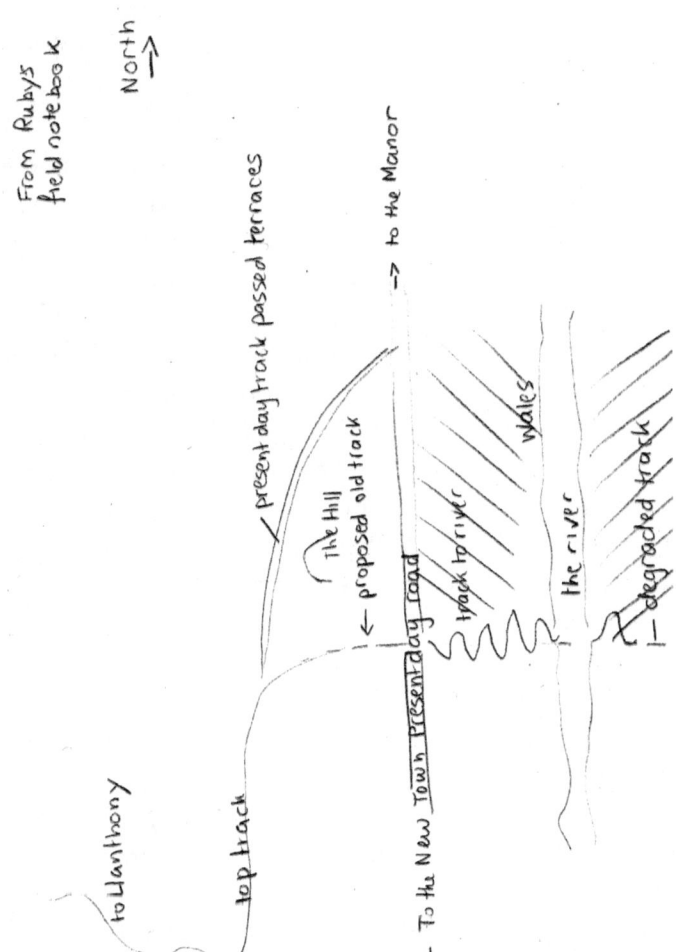

From Ruby's field notebook

North

present day track passed terraces

→ to the Manor

The Hill

← proposed old track

to Llanthony

top track

← To the New Town Present day road

track to river

wales

the river

← degraded track

"It's beautiful" exclaimed Ruby when they finally reached the bottom. The banks were steep, but there was a small narrow muddy beach by the river. The overhanging trees bent down to kiss the water. A king fisher darted into the water from a branch.

"It's amazing!" exclaimed Ruby.

"It's home," said Evan "and now it's your home too." He squeezed her hand and they kissed. "Pack horses and donkeys used to get up that steep track with goods from boats that docked here, can you believe it," he said, "it's so steep! Sheep were also taken this way down to market via boat to the New Town. The road from the New Town to Brynafon wasn't built until 1960. There was a little light gauge railway built in 1860 for the slate quarry that ran up the old track, where the road is now, but that kept getting swept away in landslides. Until 1960 the only way in and out of Brynafon was to walk, take a pony down the old railway track, more of a mountain path in places to the New Town, or take a canoe down here.

"I didn't know places like this existed," Ruby said, inhaling deeply and taking full lungs of the fresh ionised air. She looked all around her inquisitively. "This is the way Bronze Age people would have come here." She said. "Up the river, perhaps in coracles, to trade or perhaps settle, and then later the Saxons in their long boats." She looked upwards, the trees completely hid the path they had just descended on. "If the trees were not so thick, I reckon you could see your Hill from here. Especially if you were out in the middle of the river."

Evan hadn't thought about that. "I guess you're right," he said.

42

"I never thought there would be anyone who could tell me more about The Hill, than I already knew," he replied. "Remarkable!"

"I'm glad you're pleased," she smiled, "And I've got something else, you might like," she fished out a ham baguette from inside her coat. "Sunday lunch!"

"Brilliant! How did you know that was my favourite!" They both laughed. Evan took off his jacket and they sat on a rock by the river, feet swinging into the water idlily. The rain had eased and the sun had appeared making the water below them sparkle and the trees glint as if they had glitter on them like fir trees on a Christmas card.

Evan stretched out on the rock, letting the Spring sun warm his face.

"Do you reckon this rock is flat enough for us to make love on?" He enquired hopefully, "Without falling in?"

"We'll soon find out," laughed Ruby. "I just hope you can swim!"

Evan took the day off on Monday, and Ruby finished early. They took his company Land rover down to the New Town. Ruby visibly stiffened as they approached The New Town. In Brynafon she felt safe, in The New Town she clearly did not. She was wearing an old sweatshirt of Evan's. It was miles too big for, and she pulled the hood over her face as the entered the town. She could not be recognised on CCTV, and her old school coat would have been a giveaway.

Evan held her hand tightly as they left the car round the back at Bill Clackett's estate agency. He took Ruby in to meet Bill. He had briefly informed him of Ruby's history. Ruby was dressed scruffily, but Bill made no judgement on her appearance. His biggest sale in the agencies had been of the old manor at Brynafon, sold to an aging rock star in similar attire. You couldn't always tell by how a person was dressed, the details of their bank account. He held out his hand with a welcoming smile.

"Pleased to meet you," he said and meant it.

It was then a quick stop at the cheap clothing store down town. Ruby was able to get all the supplies she needed in one go.

Wellingtons, thick socks, walking boots, tights, underwear, several blouses and T shirts, a couple of fleeces, trousers, another skirt and a dress, an anorak and waterproof jacket. Evan paid by cash, and it was then a quick dash to the museum.

Ruby was enchanted by the dagger on prominent display and curator was delighted to have a visitor so interested, and obviously as well informed as Ruby. She nudged Evan, he was reluctant but had agreed to show the curator his finds from The Hill. The curator's eyes lit up instantly.

"Wonderful," he said. "I had always wondered about the dagger being the only find in Brynafon. Perhaps it was lost as a one off. But perhaps it indicated that there were other inhabitants there."

He turned the pieces over carefully, and produced an eye glass from his pocket. "May I photograph them and measure them," he asked. Evan nodded.

"They don't belong to me, and I don't own the land they were found on. I'm just storing them for an elderly resident from Brynafon."

The curator nodded. "I think they are Saxon he said, the squashed bit of metal I can't tell. They are bronze, the pin could be from a brooch, that semi-circle could be brooch or part of a buckle. This piece" he weighed the gold coin in his hand, "is gold, it is very finely worked with a Celtic type pattern, you can see there was a clasp at the back, it's definitely a brooch, and of very high status too. Gold really should be handed in, as it is treasure trove, but at least it's not been sold on the internet, and I see you've recorded all the find locations. I know it's not yours, so just tell the owner what I said, and give me a call if anything else comes to light."

Evan said he would. Ruby had kept her hoodie up the whole time, but if the curator thought it was strange he didn't say, he was used to the eccentricities of archaeology students.

They quickly exited the museum and made their way back to the car, only when they half way back to Brynafon, did Ruby push back the hood. Evan decided he'd burn the old hoodie with the rest of the cardboard boxes, better to be safe than sorry. This was a very dangerous game for Ruby indeed.

Chapter 4

It was that evening that Evan found his most significant find on The Hill. Ruby had retired to bed as she had to get up early for the bakery, and Evan was checking the sheep before turning in himself. The rain had cleared and it was a cold starry night, he looked up seeking the plough and Orion. His breath came out in clouds in the cold air. It was a wonderful night, and he wished Ruby was out enjoying it with him, but she was tucked snuggly under two quilts in the shepherd's hut fast asleep. The sheep were all settled, he thought it would be a quiet night, most had now lambed successfully, and the few left didn't look like they were going to lamb tonight. He could see puddles had formed in hollows in the grass, the moon reflecting brightly in their dark pools. As he always did after it rained, he had a quick sortie to the bottom of the Hill to check if anything had washed out of the soil, he could see nothing unusual, but would check again at first light. He then moved back up the hill to the dip under the "nose", where a pool of water always gathered after it rained. There was the pool, dark about a foot in diameter and nine inches deep, he rolled up his jacket and felt round, the water was freezing, but as always Evan methodically scanned his hand up and down from left to right, making sure he was in contact with the bottom, he was beginning to end his search, when his fingers hit something small, hard, and from experience he knew it was not a piece of mud, and probably not a stone. Carefully he fished it out, it was quite small, he was glad he hadn't missed it. He carefully washed it in the pool. He couldn't really see what it was in the dim light, small and circular, he scraped off the mud, metal was underneath.

He headed straight to the shepherd's hut. Carefully, and with trembling fingers, he washed it in the little basin. Ruby was still sleeping soundly. He took his old toothbrush and carefully scrubbed at it. The mud first shifted from the centre, and he saw a small gold circle, with a knob on one side, he carefully cleaned off the knob. He held it in front of the paraffin lamp. It was a beautiful gold ring, with a red stone set in a gold round setting. There was a simple decoration round the setting. It was a small ring, obviously, a woman's, it would only fit on his smallest finger. He looked at the stone, a red ruby or garnet, he wasn't sure, but the jewellers in The New Town would know. He would tell Owain tomorrow, which was good because he had a proposition, he'd been saving up to make to him too.

He knew he was meant to hand this ring in as treasure trove. But this one find he was going to keep, he'd pay Owain for it, of course. He knew exactly what he was going to do with the ring – he would propose to Ruby with it! He knew he hadn't known her long, but he just hoped she felt the same as he did. The thought made him shake momentarily, and his mouth went dry. He would wait for the right time, soon, fairly soon, he felt sure.

The next day was one of the most momentous days of his life, the next he hoped would be the day Ruby said "yes" to him. But tomorrow was the day he had been waiting for his whole life, it was to be the day he bought The Hill.

He knew he should be doing something sensible with his money, like saving for a deposit for a house, especially since he was an Estate Agent! But all these years he'd been saving for what he wanted most in the world, what he had wanted since he was 4 years old. To own The Hill. He hoped Ruby would not be too upset, after all it would be her future too. How could she possibly understand, he bit his lip hard, suppose he left her? It was a likely scenario for any girl, a chap buying a barren bit of Welsh hill side, fit for nothing but sheep? He thought hard, he didn't want to lose Ruby at all, that would be as bad as losing The Hill. But it couldn't wait much longer, Owain was now in his mid-eighties, and when he died, then the farm and The Hill would be sold.

Evan gave a big sigh; he would tell Ruby in the morning. He held her especially close that night as they snuggled together in the little bed, he fervently hoped it would not be their last night together. He really did love Ruby, he knew it, it hurt.

He blurted it out to her first thing in the morning, she had barely risen, her tousled black hair emerging from the duvets and blankets.

"I'm going to buy The Hill," he blurted. "I've been saving all my working life for it. I've just got enough now, and Owain is in his mid-eighties, he's had one heart attack already, if he dies it will all be sold."

Ruby looked at him, suddenly big eyed and alert, she sat up. There was not even a pause.

"Great!" She said. "Marvellous, you'll own your own piece of history! Go for it!" She gave him a hug.

He could have fainted on the spot. He couldn't believe it. What a girl Ruby was, special, incredible, precious, words failed him.

"I thought you'd be mad." He said sheepishly, his eyes had somehow gone moist.

Ruby reached out to take his hand and pulled him over to her. "I'm an archaeology student remember!"

"You're a girl in a million!" Replied Evan.

He just stood there hugging her, so very, very, relieved.

"Will he sell to you though? Owain?" She asked.

"I think so, I hope so, as it's me, he can farm here as long as he likes, and the money will buy him central heating and double glazing, and the things he needs to stay at the farm, he never wants to leave you know."

Ruby nodded.

"Shall we go to the Dragon and Dagger this evening, if it all pans out?" He asked.

"Good idea." Ruby hopped out of bed, "I better get a move on or I'll be late for work."

The day seems to drag. He shut up the shop at 5p.m. and promptly left for Owain's. He let himself by the broken back door as he always did. He went through the dilapidated kitchen with its Aga, Welsh dresser and handmade slate worktops, and into Owain's front room, as he had so often in the past. He could not see Owain, the high winged back chair where Owain always sat, hid the small farmer completely. Meg his sheep dog looked up briefly from in front of the fire, then settled down with her head on her paws again.

"Hello Meg," Evan said, bending down to pat her soft head, Meg's tail gave a few wags, before settling again. It had been a cold hard day again for both dog and master.

"Aye, there boy," Owain said. He was puffing at his pipe, the curls of smoke coming from above the wing back chair. A mug of tea, with a sheep dog on it, and yesterday's newspaper beside him on the small table. There was no television, just the coal fire and Meg to keep him company.

Evan sat down on the old chair opposite him.

"Cold today," Evan said in Welsh. Owain was a native Welsh speaker, and they always spoke Welsh together. It was good practice Evan thought, for when he had to negotiate for the hill farmers who were often selling up nowadays.

"Oh, Aye, wish Spring would make its mind up and get on with it." Owain took another puff on his pipe. "What can I do for you boy, then?"

In truth Evan popped in every day on his way back from work to see that Owain was alright, and Owain always said the same thing.

Evan rummaged in his pocket.

"Got something to show you," He said. He unwrapped the gold ring from his hankie in his pocket, the red jewel glowed like a hot ember in the fire light.

Owain took it carefully and peered at it from different angles, his glasses perched precariously on his nose. The rims held together with sticky tape.

"Did you find it at the same place, under the nose on The Hill?"

"I did," said Evan. "And this piece I want to keep, so can I buy it off you please?"

Owain gave a puff of his pipe, and closed his eyes shrewdly.

"This wouldn't be for someone special, to propose to her, would it be boy?"

Really Owain could be very wily sometimes.

"Yes, it would, I've not popped the question yet. So, don't say anything about this find. I just hope she says yes." He sighed.

"Nice girl, that Ruby of yours," said Owain, "Reminds me a lot of my poor girl, I had. Not in looks of course, my Megan was blonde, with big breasts." Owain indicated in front of him. By the looks of it Megan's breasts had grown during the years along with his imagination somewhat.

Evan had to grin, Owain's dog Meg was named after the late unfortunate Megan as well.

Owain continued, "But a nice manner to her, tries to help others, not stuck up like some folks despite the accent."

"So, you approve?" Asked Evan.

"Of course, I do boy, you'll have to do better than a shepherd's hut though soon, can't have a girl like that living in the shepherd's hut all her life."

"I know," said Evan with a sigh.

"And I don't want anything for that ring now, that's my gift to the two of you." Owain gave the ring back to Evan, who stowed it safely back in his hankie in his pocket.

Evan argued for a bit but Owain was set.

"I just hope you like my other proposal as much," Evan ventured.

"Spit it out boy," said Owain, "I'm not getting any younger and my leek casserole will be done soon."

"Well, that's kind of what it's about," said Evan. He took a deep breath and paused slightly. "I want to buy The Hill from you, just the field. I know the market value and I can offer you that, you could still farm there, use it all you want of course. It's just that legally I will own The Hill. The money should be able to buy you central heating, double glazing, and do up the place a bit, so you can stay here in comfort, how about it? I'll get all the paper work and law stuff done for you, so you won't have to do anything except sign."

Owain thought for a bit, and puffed on his pipe. The fire embers glowed and spat intermittently.

"Yep, it's cold here for me and Meg now I'm getting older, and I've kind of thought of you as the son I never had all these years," Owain said slowly.

Evan was amazed and very touched, he had never really known what Owain had thought of him, or even if he liked him, Owain had never really shown it, although from the age of eight Evan had worked side by side with Owain, listening and learning. Like father and son, through rain, sleet, snow and blasting icy winds. Working together quietly side by side to protect and nurture Owain's small flock.

Owain stuck his hand out to Evan, "It's yours," he said.

It was a bit of a party that night at the Dragon and Dagger. Ruby and Evan dined well on a homemade steak and ale pie, washed down with a red wine for Ruby and a coke for Evan. Evan thought he couldn't have been happier, only perhaps when Ruby said yes. She looked happy though he thought, she sparkled like a jewel in the light of the roaring fire. She had filled out just slightly since he first met her, she was less gaunt, and her cheeks had a rosy glow now. The black make up was less pronounced and her hair had grown about an inch, framing her face in a softer way.

They held hands across the table.

"Are you happy here Ruby?" He asked. "I'd imagined you would have finished that degree and going on archaeological digs somewhere exotic and hot like Egypt." Ruby, he thought, for all the world looked like an Egyptian Queen on one of those Egyptian friezes.

Ruby smiled. "That's what I thought too, I'd intended something like that. But hopefully Professor Forster will come through so I can take my degree exams, and as for the rest of it, well I suppose I should thank my Dad really. Instead of being off somewhere exotic, I had to run... but I found you, The Hill, and the community here. You don't get a sense of friendship like that in a large city. It's like we're all a part of a big family, it was like that at the convent school too. Ups and downs, but in it together. I have a job, not what I intended, but I have my plans," she smiled, "I'd very much like to publish my findings on The Hill, and perhaps if I get lucky write a book about it. I can't do much about the weather, but I do have you to keep warm with!"

She held his hand under the tightly. Yes, Ruby was quite a girl.

Evan's friends descended on the bar, Pete, Dave and his girlfriend Sian. Sian had quickly tired of Pete and moved on to Dave. Evan beckoned them over to tell them the news about his forth coming ownership of The Hill. They all raised a glass to celebrate. There was a loud clanking of glasses and quite a lot of spilt drink to go with it. They didn't understand Evan's compulsion, but knew it was something Evan had always wanted, so they were pleased for him.

"And what do you think of it Red?" Enquired Pete. "You're officially going out with the looney here who's bought The Hill, told you should have been going out with me! Bet you thought, there's a smart guy, works for an estate agent, bound to buy a nice warm little house for me, but oh no, he buys that God forsaken piece of bulging hillside!"

Ruby laughed. Her old nickname of Red had somehow stuck, she didn't mind. It meant if her Dad came looking for a girl called Ruby, and she was known as Red, he was less likely to get a favourable reply.

"I think it's great, not everyone owns a bit of history, and I fully intend to put a few test pits in when it gets warmer."

"Test pits?" Asked Pete.

"Yes, holes where you see if you can find any archaeology."

"Treasure seeking!" Said Dave.

"Not quite," answered Ruby, "but you never know!"

Chapter 5

The next week was eventful in a number of ways. Firstly, a box arrived for Evan delivered to Bill Clackett's Estate Agency in The New Town. Monday, after finishing early, Evan went to collect it. It was a largish box, not too heavy. It was just addressed to "Bill Clackett's Estate Agency" in a printed hand. It was a recycled box and had contained copier paper. He noticed the post mark said Bath, not Bristol. Bill Clackett hadn't ordered anything, and he knew this was the box for Ruby, which had Evan said might be arriving.

"Glad you're here," said Bill. He had a mug of tea in an old battered brown mug waiting for Evan when he arrived and a three-quarter eaten packet of custard cremes. He offered the biscuits to Evan who took one.

Bill, he couldn't help notice was looking tired, and a bit worried.

"What's the matter," asked Evan, after he had dutifully devoured his biscuit.

"Well, we're a bit quiet business wise, both of us, picked up a bit, now it's slumped again. The problem is we just don't have the properties coming on to the market, especially for the young couples starting off and wanting to raise a family." Said Bill.

Evan nodded. "Right enough," he said. "Someone has to die before something is available in Brynafon nowadays. I'm doing most of my business out at the isolated farm steads." Evan was not too worried; it was the best part of his job going out in the country and visiting the farmers. Not that they were always easy to deal with, but his love of sheep helped. Bill Clackett's Estate Agency didn't just sell property, it also auctioned property, mainly farms and old farm buildings, and managed a variety of rentals, mainly holiday lets for farmers, so going out to the farms was quite a regular occurrence, hence Evan had the firms 4x4.

"Precisely," said Bill between gulps of tea. "What we need is some new housing stock, particularly in Brynafon. The school was built in the 1860s on land that had been owned by the manor farm, so I was wondering whether this week you could take a trip up there, and try to charm Jed Buggins to sell his land opposite the school, for housing, would probably fit three or four houses on that site, stopping in line with the school. That's if you don't object, now you're the prospective owner of The Hill behind it."

"Not at all," said Evan, he wished he'd thought of it. Still that was why Bill Clackett was the boss, and he was just the apprentice.

"Good, so I'll wait to hear from you then, try to charm the old fellow will you. We, and Brynafon, desperately need those houses. I'll then get planning permission, and we'll get Johnny to build them for us, keep it as in house as possible for maximum profit." Bill gave Evan a figure he could haggle to. "You'll be needing housing for you and that girl of yours soon."

Evan nodded. He had told Bill Clackett confidentially about his hopes of an engagement to Ruby. Bill was family to him and as much as a father to him as Owain was.

"I know," sighed Evan. "I'm not sure how I'll afford it, especially with buying The Hill."

"You're not regretting your decision?" Enquired Bill, downing the last of the biscuits, the crumpled biscuit wrapper speaking volumes for the empty state of the Estate Agency business.

"Hell, no," replied Evan. "I just want Ruby, and somewhere to live with her as well!"

"Good," said Bill. "I liked what I saw of her, I'll get the missus to invite you both round for Sunday lunch, we can all get to know her better then."

"That would be great," enthused Evan. Mrs Clackett was a superb cook.

"Good, I'll let you know then. I'm also negotiating for a bit of land down here by the railway, so hopefully we'll have some movement in the housing soon. It'll warm up and with more day light soon, and then it'll be busy, and hopefully we'll have something to sell them."

"Amen" to that, replied Evan.

Ruby was delighted that evening when Evan appeared with the box. He noticed the back wall of the shepherd's hut was now adorned with a grid that plotted all the finds on the Hill.

"Been busy?" He enquired,

"Yes," she said, "now give me that box!" He teased he with it a minute before relenting. She fell on it eagerly ripping it open. Inside was a letter written on some lined paper it read:

"Dear Precious,

This is what I managed to salvaged for you. I had occasion to visit Bath Archaeology this week, so posted it from there, which I thought safer.

I hope this finds you well and happy.

It was easier than I thought, I just asked your floor cleaner to let me into your room, as I needed to get back some books, I had leant you, so it aroused no suspicion. I found your file, laptop and memory stick where you said. I also managed to smuggle out the Archaeology handbook, Theories, Methods and Practice and a couple of other books for you. I have added my own latest book out as a present for you: "Reading the Past" which I hope you find useful."

Evan picked up the book, it had a blue cover and a picture of some standing stones on the front against a sunset or sunrise. Dr. Forster had inscribed the book to Ruby on the front piece. The back of the jacket had a photograph of said Dr. Elizabeth Mary Forster on it. A lady with a round face beamed out at him. She had on round silver rimmed glasses, with two very blue eyes behind them. Her round face was framed by a short blonde bob to her cheeks, and a blonde fringe. She had a kind smile and apple red cheeks. Evan thought she looked about fifty. Her clothing consisted of a stripy home knitted scarf and an orange woolly jumper with what looked like it alpaca heads on it. Clearly, she was an eccentric dresser, and it was obvious that her academic work was what was important to her. There was a bookshelf crammed to over flowing with books behind her in the photo, a window into a garden, where he could see a cherry tree in blossom. A small wooden rustic door to off to her left behind her, and a small round table beside some type of flint implement on it and a lampstand. The photograph was obviously taken at her home, which appeared to be a small cottage. The writing underneath chartered her academic success. Clearly Dr. Elizabeth Mary Forster was an academic high flyer.

The letter continued:

"I also managed to sneak your violin out, I know you loved it so, not the case unfortunately. I was wearing a capacious coat at the time, and apart from the books I put everything under my coat. It was quite exciting really, so no one suspected I was helping you.

I have also entered you for your exams in Chester. This seemed the safest option for you.

All my love

F"

With a screech of delight, Ruby unwrapped the violin from its abundant bubble wrapping. She had a brief bow stroke across the strings, turned the pegs a little, and then a flurry of amazing virtuoso sound came tumbling from the strings, filling the shepherd's hut entirely. It was as vibrant, exciting and as brilliant as Ruby was.

"Spring, by Vivaldi! "She laughed. "I thought it was appropriate."

Evan was amazed. How could Ruby be so talented! It sounded like a professional!

"I didn't know you could play the violin!" he said. How much more did he not know about her!

"Yes," She laughed again. "I'm going to see if the Pastor wants me to play at church occasionally, it would be a good thank you for him, he's been so kind to me. There was lots of music and singing at the convent, and we all had to learn an instrument, so I learnt the violin. I passed grade eight at sixteen with honours. There was no television at the convent school, so there was plenty of time to practice."

Ruby eagerly gathered up the books and file and stacked them. "I've got some catching up to do on my studies," she said happily.

Spring had truly arrived at last! It was a balmy 17 degrees. The daffodils were out in abundance. The pointed wild ones nodding their heads on the side of the road, and enchanting small tete at tete ones swaying in the hanging baskets that were outside many of the cottages. The cherry trees were in full bloom, the wild yellow ones on the hillsides and several pink ornamental ones in the back gardens. The birds were all busy, whizzing round with twigs in their mouths to build their nests, and bees were going frantically at the flowers. It was Spring alright.

It was quiet at work so Evan shut the shop for an hour and went to find Ruby. This was the day to go out in the countryside and see Jed Buggins. Apart from Ruby's one rather frightening trip to The New Town, Ruby had not set foot outside Brynafon since she had first arrived. Evan was wondering when a girl with an enquiring mind like Ruby would decide she'd had enough of the quiet rural backwater of Brynafon, and what to leave it, and him.

He found Ruby planting out seeds he had bought her in the vegetable patch, he had made at the back of the shepherd's hut for her. He had carefully fenced off the area with chicken wire from the roving sheep and rabbits, and dug over a large vegetable bed, manuring in spadesful of manure from the sheep. Ruby had expressed an interest in growing some vegetables for cooking, many of the older ladies were good cooks in Brynafon, and they chatted in the bakery about recipes to her. Ruby had had some experience of helping the nuns in their kitchen garden at her convent school, the convent and school had been self-sufficient in vegetables. The nuns did not like to waste money by buying vegetables in. All the girls had had to volunteer for chores, and Ruby had chosen to help in the kitchen gardens. She had not had much chance to cook, and food at university mainly consisted of microwave meals, so she was keen to learn.

Evan had bought her peas, broad beans, potato tubers, onions and garlic, leeks, broccoli, cauliflower, carrots and cabbages to sow. Ruby was leaning on the spade, her hair tied back with an old bit of curtain fabric. She wore jeans, and an old t-shirt of Evan's. Even like that she looked gorgeous he thought.

"Have you finished?" He asked.

"Just," she said wiping her face, "I finished early at the bakery today so had time to get the planting done."

"Good" he said. "We're off on a jaunt on Estate Agency business to see Jed Buggins at the Manor Farm," he said. "So, get cleaned up and best gear on, I'll get you a quick cuppa."

"Who?" She asked.

"I'll explain in Land Rover," he replied.

Twenty minutes later they were in the Land Rover heading north out of the village, up a bumpy track that lead to Jed Buggins place. It was a further twenty minutes up the pot holed and muddy track to the farm. Ruby could see why Evan needed a company Land Rover.

"This must have been fun on your motorbike," she commented.

"It was," smiled Evan, "that first trip up here on my motorbike to clinch the sale of Manor Farm. I and the bike nearly didn't make it, and I slid about wildly twice, when I got back to the office, to report to Bill I was covered in thick mud from head to foot. The remaining customers there fell about laughing! Mind you when Bill heard we landed the deal he gave me the rest of the day off, and told me to go home to get cleaned up!" On the proceeds of that sale Bill got the Land Rover for us, he opened the Brynafon office and I got to be manager of it. You know I really think I'm a lucky chap, that sale, the office, having you as my girlfriend (and fiancée he hoped soon) and The Hill! Yes, I have a lot to thank Jed Buggins for."

"He was my first really big sale, I was eighteen," said Evan. "Bill should have handled it but he was busy with four other clients, when this guy walked into the office, we only had the one office at the New Town then. He parked his Rolls on double yellow lines outside the office, the Rolls was quite something I can tell you. Sauntered into the shop, hands in pockets, scruffy jeans, and an old shirt on, said did we have anything isolated on the market? The Manor Farm had just been released for sale by probate, so I headed the way on the motorbike I had then up to Brynafon and Manor Farm. I couldn't believe it, when Jed said he'd have it. He didn't even go in, just had a quick word with his chauffeur and the deal was closed! Bill and I never thought he'd go through and buy it but he did. He's been there ever since."

"What's he like? This Jed Buggins." Asked Ruby.

Jed or Jedburgh Buggins to give him his proper name was rather rudely known by the locals as "The bugger at the manor". He was a recluse, a former rock star, lead guitarist and singer with the band The Roaring Rainbows. The band, a strange fusion of rock and peace movement hippy, had had multiple platinum selling records, before eventually fading away as their crew died off mainly due to drugs, alcohol and associated accidents and diseases.

"That's rather sad," commented Ruby. "So, he'd hardly ever seen now in the village, I certainly haven't seen him."

"Once a week he sends his driver out to get provisions in the old Rolls. God knows how he gets it up and down this track, and that's about it."

"Oh," said Ruby "Let's just hope he agreeable to parting with some of his land then."

"I hope so, that's why you're along to charm him Ruby!" Evan laughed. "I hear he was quite one for the ladies in his day, I was doing a bit of research with information I could use as a lever with him."

Ruby frowned. "I'm not sure I've ever charmed anyone in my life!" She said.

"You charmed me!" Commented Evan.

Ruby did look good as she stepped out onto the uneven terracing in front of the small Victorian manor. Short red tight-fitting dress, red lipstick, dark Cleopatra eyeliner and glossy straight black hair. She looked every part the rock star chick.

"That must be the Rolls!" She said "Wow!"

The Rolls was certainly a sight. It was painted silver and still shined to perfection weekly. But it wasn't the silver that drew the eye but the rainbow painted the length of the car ending in a fiery tail over the rear end of the car.

"That must stand out in Brynafon!" She smiled.

"Oh, it does!" Commented Evan. "Let's ring the bell and see if he'll invite us in?"

It was the driver come butler who opened the door. A small old guy about five foot two with bandy legs with wispy grey hair wearing jeans and an old white shirt without a collar.

"Oh hello," he said. "It's you, the lad estate agent, although you've matured into a man since I saw you last, and less covered with mud!"

He glanced towards the Land Rover.

"Just the job," he said. "I've been telling Jed we must get one of those. The Rolls won't last much longer, been on its last legs for quite some time. Reliable, are they?"

"Oh yes," said Evan thankful for the opening gambit. "Very, all the farmers round here swear by them. If you want new I can give you the name and address of the dealer in the New Town, where this one came from, or if you want second hand, I'll introduce you to my mate Dave at Brynafon garage, who will keep an eye open for you and check anything out for you, you like."

"Yep, that would be handy, thanks, name's Nick." They shook hands. "I'll see if Jed's free, come through here."

They were in. The first thing Ruby noticed was the motorbike in the hall. It was on a pedestal and was an old one similar to the one her father had, but of a more laid back variety. A Harley Davidson she thought. This one was shiny silver, and had a Union Jack and Stars and Stripes pendant on the back of it.

"Admiring the bike?" Asked Nick.

"Yes," said Ruby.

"The band rode Route 66 in America, this was Jed's bike."

Nick lead them to a well-proportioned sitting room. The furniture was an eclectic mix of leather chesterfields, chintz sofas and tartan high back chairs. A fire was burning steadily in the large fireplace. Nick indicated them to sit down. A black and white cat sauntered over from her place on a sunny windowsill to rub and purr against Ruby's legs. Ruby leant down to stroke the purring creature, and tickle it under its chin. It immediately rolled over on its back with legs in the air. It reminded Ruby of the convent cat Maestro.

"That's Molly, she just wandered in one day, goodness knows where she came from, there are no houses or farms for miles around. She just sorted adopted us and us her I didn't get your names?" added Nick.

"Evan from Bill Clackett's Estate Agency and my friend here is Ruby, locally known as Red."

Nick nodded. He was gone about three minutes. The cat took the opportunity to have its tummy rubbed. The purrs went up a notch. Nick appeared at the door again.

"He says come through; he's working in the studio." They crossed the hallway with its central stairs again and found themselves in a room of similar proportions. It was chock full of cables, amplifiers, a piano, a keyboard, drums, several guitars, and sheets of music paper.

"Take a pew," said Nick indicating to a couple of bars stools. "drinks?"

"Tea please, no sugars for us, thank you." Said Evan. This was looking more promising by the minute.

Jed looked up from the piano and idled over. He too was dressed in jeans, cowboy boots, and had a red and white shirt on. He was medium height, with brown lined skinned, a shock of white hair that went in all directions and the bluest eyes Ruby had ever seen. Jed held out his hand.

"The pleasure's all mine," he said surveying Ruby appreciatively. "What can I do for you, Nick tells me you're the young lad with the motorbike that sold me the place, my memory not as good as it used to be with faces."

Evan had a quick glance round. The place didn't look like much had been done to it since Jed had moved in, and it had been pretty run down then. The curtains looked newish but looked like they had come from another bigger house, as they draped way over the floor. The electronics looked about ten years old, the piano was a Steinbeck and behind the piano on the wall was a huge picture of the band as they were in their heyday. Album covers covered the wall, and there was a platinum, couple of gold LPs and a silver on the wall.

Evan quickly surmised money was short. That might make the negotiations a good deal easier.

Jed saw Ruby looking around in wonder.

"Here," he said leading her towards the huge photograph of the band on the wall. "That's me in the centre, I was lead guitarist and vocalist with The Roaring Rainbows. That's Rick the other guitarist to my right. Bobo on keyboards, Bash on Drums, Freddie on bass, and Benedict on the violin."

"You had a violinist!" Said Ruby in amazement. "Sure," responded Jed. "Why do you play?"

"Yes, the violin, but mainly classical." Said Ruby.

"He's the only one who survives now," said Jed sadly. "Benedict, he wasn't like us, he was a public-school boy, we were all EastEnders. He went to play in an orchestra after we finished. Bobo died of an overdose, silly bugger, he was the first to go, followed by Rick who drank himself to death, Freddie got liver cancer and Bash thought he could fly one day and launched himself out of a top storey penthouse flat." Jed shook his head. "All gone now," he said again sadly. "Nick here was our driver, he used to be flat jockey before he had a bad horse-riding accident, that was when we met, in bar in York when he was downing his troubles. He needed another job, we needed a driver quickly, ours had just been hauled down the nick for drink and drugs driving and countless road violations. Nick's been with me ever since. Yeah after it all went south and Bash died, I was in quite a state, Nick said we needed to move away, have a fresh start somewhere quiet and isolated. He'd been racing at Chepstow and vaguely knew this area and liked it. So, one day he bundled me in the Roller and we came down here, saw this place, it was all the money I had left and Nick said we should buy it. So, I did, reckon Nick saved my life, been here ever since, I compose a bit, sell a few songs here and there, keeps us going.

What about you young lady, you're not from round these parts are you, what are you doing here?"

"Much the same as you," replied Ruby "had to get away somewhere quiet and found Evan here." She smiled.

Jed seemed quite charmed.

Nick had fetched the tea and a cup for Jed and himself, and they wandered through to the drawing room again and sat in front of the fire amicably. Molly joined them still purring by the fire and sprawled out comfortably.

"Don't get many visitors here," said Jed after the tea was finished. "So, what's your business with me?"

Evan explained about the need for housing in the village, and how Bill Clackett thought he could get planning permission for three opposite the school. Two three bed semis, and a detached four. Evan had buyers for them already if Jed agreed, Jed wouldn't have to do a thing, just sign. Evan offered a figure.

"Yeah, it's bad about young people not been able to afford to live in the villages they were raised," Said Jed. "And who owns the land abutting mine, will they object?" Asked Jed.

"I do," said Evan. "At least I am in the process of buying The Hill, and Owain Jones the sheep farmer owns the rest of the high land adjoining yours. No problem there, I can assure you."

"Ah yes, I heard about a looney boy who was obsessed about The Hill and slept out nights there." Said Jed.

Evan laughed, "Yep, that was me," he said. "Now I own it! I still sleep there though in a shepherd's hut. Although I'll be needing somewhere more substantial for the Winter now I have Ruby."

"You're a lucky man," said Jed casting a wistfully eye at Ruby. "If he doesn't treat you well young Ruby, you know where I am!" Jed still had a heck of a smile when he used it. Ruby could see that his groupies would have adored him.

Ruby smiled, Jed must have been in his late seventies. There were a few more further questions from Nick, it was soon apparent he was the real brains behind the outfit and kept the show on the road.

"We've got some barns out to the back there, could be doing something with those too," Said Nick. Jed nodded. "I'll show you."

Jed and Nick showed them a range of barns in a U shape.

"Well, there are various possibilities," said Evan. "Holiday cottages, although this area is a bit over run with them and they are not all letting any longer. Creating housing to rent or buy. There's a couple of families I could think of who really want to get into small holding and farming, who would die for a place like this, where they could run some livestock and grow some vegetables. Another lass I know wants to set up a trekking centre, it would be ideal."

Nick nodded to Jed.

"OK," said Jed, "We like the sound of those last two options would be nice to have some youngsters livening up the place and running around, never had any children myself, lots of young ladies of course in my time. I like the sound of getting the farm up and running again, making it working and helping the locals too. Money would come in handy too, Nick says we need to replace the Rolls with a Land Rover....Tell you what, you bring the paperwork along, and Ruby you come and play your violin for me, and we'll have a deal."

Jed and Evan shook hands on the deal.

Evan squeezed Ruby's hand tightly back in the Land Rover. If Ruby said yes to him, he would be the luckiest man in the world, and right now he was a pretty lucky and grateful fellow. Jed and Nick were good guys at heart, if only all of life was that simple.

Chapter 6

The deal had gone down, as they say. Evan and Ruby had gone back to Manor Farm two days later with the paperwork. Ruby had played her violin brilliantly and Jed had been very impressed. In fact, he had asked her to come and jam with him every week. Ruby had said she would love to, Evan was happy to drive her up and back and keep an eye on proceedings, it would be handy as there was a lot of planning permissions and decisions to be discussed and made still. Evan believed in working hard to make things work, his parents had instilled in him a strong work ethic, although, he smiled to himself, it had not been apparent when he was at school.

Ruby had invited Jed and Nick down to the pub with them on Friday, but Jed said he kept away from pub's nowadays. Nick had nodded firmly. Evan smiled and said the good Pastor would be reciting Halleluiahs over that one. But Jed agree to come down to the bakery, Ruby thought it was the renowned bacon rolls that had probably swung the decision, Evan thought it was probably Ruby.

So, the next week saw the Rolls conspicuously parked outside the bakery, while Jed and Nick were chomping into a late breakfast of sizzling bacon rolls, loads of ketchup and a large pot of tea.

"Just like the old days," remarked Jed.

"Better," said Nick. He sighed and stretched his achy joints in the sun.

Owain was also at the table, grabbing a morning bacon roll, a very late breakfast for him as he was want to do. It was handy for him living across from the bakery, he didn't like cooking at the best of times.

The men were in full conversation. It was Ruby who had introduced them to each other. Jed was admiring Owain's chickens that were loitering with intent the other side of the picket fencing that kept them out of the outside paved area of the café, hoping the women with toddlers would throw them titbits, which they frequently did.

The chickens were not the run of the mill brown Rhode Island Red's normally associated with farms, but these were showy girls, large ginger fluffy chickens, with engaging, happy personalities, Orpington's mainly Buff and Lemon varieties. Owain had inherited their forbearers from Manor Farm when the last Lord passed away. The Lord had kept a number of fancy breeds, but the native breed Orpington's with their large size, large feather covering and free ranging capabilities, had thrived and prospered in the village. Owain now had a sizable flock and many of the villagers their own smaller flocks. Jed and Nick had been admiring them and especially the young chicks that were dutifully following their mothers' around. Nick had been saying how useful it would be to have some up and Manor Farm, and not have to trudge down to the village just for eggs. Owain, who had been wondering what to do with them all, as the village shop would not be needing quite so many eggs, and was happy to sell some to Jed and Nick.

Owain was telling them to make sure they were locked up at night away from the foxes. Nick had looked after horses for most of his young life, and said he would be well up to caring for the chickens, they could live in one of the old stables.

"Aye, there's some for you Ruby too, love." Said Owain. Ruby had wandered over to see if they needed more rolls, all three decided they were ravenous. "I'll bring them up as soon as Evan has made a coop for them," he said. Ruby was delighted, she'd always wanted chickens. Owain got a big kiss on the cheek.

"I don't get one of those!" Said Jed enviously.

Ruby laughed, "I've got my reputation to think of now I've got a live-in boyfriend," she said with a wink towards Owain.

"Fine lass, that!" said Owain, as soon as Ruby had left the table. "He's a lucky lad that Evan!"

"He is indeed." Sighed Jed.

So, after a second round of rolls, and Owain having sat down on the day for as a long time as he could remember, mother and chicks were boxed up in a cardboard box in the bakery, and given a stately ride back to the Manor in the Rolls Royce with Jed holding the box tightly over the bumpy track.

"As soon as the initial money comes in, we'll get you that Land Rover," said Jed.

"Good," said Jed, "I don't think my old joints will take much more of this, or the Rolls."

That first meeting was the auspicious start of an unlikely friendship between Owain, Jed and Nick. As Owain explained when Evan called in him to see he after work as he did every day.

"He's not a bad chap that Jed," said Owain thoughtfully, "and me and Nick were able to discuss the animals, been a jockey in his early life you know." Evan nodded his head.

"You know, Jed and I had a lot more in common than I'd have ever thought. He had a fiancée once too, his was called Eileen, Irish lass. His was killed too, car crash, broke his heart he said, just like mine did, he said although there were lots of lasses afterwards, there were none like his Eileen, and he never met one he wanted to settle down with like her. Aye, funny how life goes isn't it.

Yes, he's going be coming down the café regularly now he's going get a Land Rover, and he'll give me a call and we'll meet up for a bacon roll, it'll be nice." He said. "He's even invited me up to the Manor for dinner, fancy that!"

Evan smiled. He was so pleased for Owain, and for Jed and Nick. He had been the only person Owain regularly talked to over all these years.

"That'll be great," said Evan. Owain was nodding off in the chair a smile on his face.

When Evan came home from work Ruby was digging again, this time not in their new vegetable patch, but the test pits on The Hill she had talked about at the pub. Evan noticed the night before new markings had appeared on her map of The Hill. Three test pits were shown at the top, three in the middle, one slightly further down from the hollow under "the nose" of The Hill, and three at the bottom. Evan was relieved to see Ruby was not digging on the bulge of The Hill itself. He wasn't quite sure about how he felt about his precious

Hill being dug into, not even by Ruby. He had quizzed her about it that night.

She assured him she would not be digging into The Hill itself.

"Oh no," she said reassuringly. "I was going to ask your permission before digging anything anyway. I certainly won't be digging into The Hill itself. That's what the Victorian early antiquarians did, and the barrows collapsed, sometimes they found artefacts and didn't record it properly, or didn't realise its significance, like sherds of pottery from funeral urns, and sometimes they missed the centre of found nothing at all. Besides it would be far too dangerous, it could destabilise The Hill entirely, like what happened at Silbury Hill in Wiltshire, when the hill there started to collapse because early archaeologists had made tunnels in it. It would need a proper excavation team with wooden props to stabilise The Hill. Then you might not find anything, it could just be a cairn of stones for example. Archaeology is a very destructive process. You only want to dig if you have to. No, just doing the test pits is all I need to do right now. There is an exam question where I have talk about my findings and methods on a site, The Hill is going to be my site. If that's all alright with you, of course?" Ruby looked at him anxiously with those big dark lash fringed eyes of her.

"That's fine," Evan assured her, he was really quite curious to see what might be in the pits too.

The pits turned out to be only a foot square. The first three only went down and inch to two inches before they hit bed rock and were above the top of the bulge of The Hill. They yielded a rusty nail, probably Victorian,

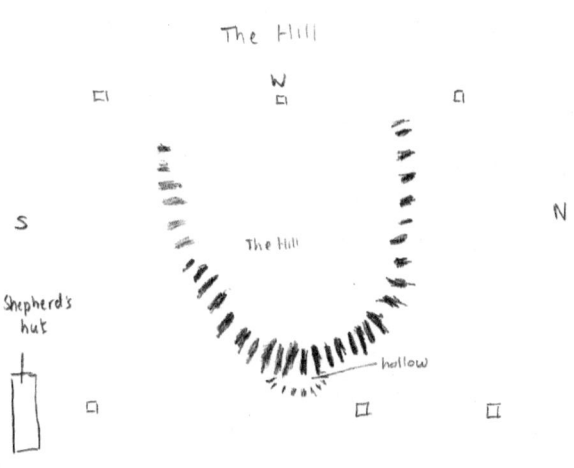

The Hill

W

S

N

The Hill

hollow

Shepherd's
hut

☐ Excavation pits

fence line

a small amount of barbed wire and a piece of red baler twine.

"Hmm," said Evan, "Not what I'd hoped for!"

"I think will get more interesting as I get down the slope, at least that's what I hope," laughed Ruby. "But it has proved it's point, no significant finds on top of The Hill, so it is unlikely that the gold and bronze items you found, have come from above The Hill. Therefore, they are likely to becoming from The Hill itself. At least that's what I hope I might be able to prove." Explained Ruby.

Evan nodded, it was good reasoning, he wished he'd thought about going about his search of The Hill in a logical fashion like that, instead he'd just meandered over it, looking in the puddle under the nose, and sometimes at the base of the field by the fencing. Finding nothing, it appeared didn't mean one had not found anything out.

It came as a complete shock. The phone call, one minute he was sitting casually at his at work watching the rain lash against the window, and the next it was complete panic and utter despair.

The caller said only two words, but those words turned Evan's heart to beat frantically:

"He's coming!" The caller had a muted hushed tone to his voice, and it was a voice he recognised, it was Bill Clackett. It only meant one thing. Ruby's Dad was on his way to Brynafon. It was a stroke of good fortune that Evan got the call at all.

Later Evan heard the full story from Bill. It had been four o'clock and the New Town Estate Agency office was deserted apart from Bill. It had suddenly started to rain hard outside, one of those heavy thundery sudden April showers, shoppers had hurried for cover and hurried home. Bill had his head down pouring over the plans for the new houses in Brynafon, when he heard the bell on the door go. A guy about five foot ten was entering the shop, he was dressed in black motorcycle leathers. Bill glanced behind the guy through the window to see a dark coloured classic bike parked on double yellow lines outside the shop. He was just about to tell the guy that he could park round the back legally, but what the hell it was raining and no traffic wardens were likely to be about. The guy removed his helmet. He was in his fifties with white hair, a moustache and dark eyes. In that instant, there was something about that guy, something icy cold and menacing. Bill automatically felt for the panic button under his desk. Surely the guy wasn't going to rob him, there was hardly any cash on the premises.

The guy smiled and walked over calmly. He had an educated slightly plumy accent.

"I'm wondering if you've had a young girl in here trying to rent a flat from you. She's slim with black hair. Only she's a runaway, and her poor parents are distraught with worry about her, her poor mother is almost suicidal with grief. I've offered to help the family to try and find her, any news at all would be of terrific comfort to them."

The guy was all charm and concern, Bill Clackett did not believe a word of it. He told him rather stiffly that he did not deal with the lower end of the market.

"I sent him to Dodgy Dick's at the other end of town!" Grinned Bill, Evan and him would laugh about that bit later when it was all over.

Evan grabbed the keys to the office, and locking the door rushed into the street in the rain. Where was Ruby? He had to warn her. Bill had known enough not to make the call to Evan first thing after the guy had left. He had waited for another call to come and made a quick call himself before phoning Evan. Ruby's father could be here by now. He glanced up and down the street, there was no sign of a motorbike, it was getting quite dark with the storm. He rushed up towards the bakery, they normally finished at four, sometimes earlier if everything was sold. Had Ruby finished early, or was she still clearing up? Would she walk out of the shop and straight into the arms of her father? There were no lights on at the bakery. He dashed through Owain's gate and straight up The Hill, remembering to glance behind him to make sure no one had seen him. He scrambled behind the sheep, who were riding out the storm beside the stone wall. Crawling on all fours, his suit and good shoes covered in mud, his hair plastered to his face. He was panting more in shock than anything else when he reached the shepherd's huts, there were no lights on. Was Ruby lying dead inside. Please, please God, don't let Ruby be dead, he prayed like he never had in his life before. He was almost sobbing. The wet icy rain stung his face, he hardly noticed it. He flung open the shepherd's hut door.....

Two shotguns stabbed him in the face.

"What the hell!" He exclaimed. "Ruby? Owain?"

"And me," said Dave from behind him. Evan blinked into the gloom.

"Come in, shut the door quickly!" Barked Owain. "He might still be around, did you see anyone, or his motorbike?" Asked Owain.

"No, no-one" said Evan. "Blimey Owain, you two could have blown my head off, and Ruby, what are you doing with a gun! Do you know how to use it!"

"There, there," said Owain, speaking to him like when he a boy, and upset for being dragged of The Hill.

"Well we didn't shoot you did we! Stop making a fuss, yes and Ruby knows how to use it."

"My father taught me," said Ruby.

There was so much about Ruby, he didn't know about thought Evan. He hated guns, and had never wanted to handle one.

"I had a spare shotgun so I gave it to Ruby, I think she should keep it up here, just in case," said Owain.

"But how did you know her Father was here, and Dave what are you doing here?" Asked Evan. He suddenly felt quite shaky and a little bit sick. He sat down on the bed. "I got a call from Bill to say your Dad was on his way Ruby, but how did you all know?" Enquired Evan.

Ruby and Evan still had their guns trained firmly on the door.

"Well it's all thanks to your friend Dave here," Owain nodded approvingly at Dave.

Dave joined Evan sitting on the bed. Dave worked as a mechanic in the Brynafon garage. It was the first building one came to in Brynafon from The New Town. "I had my head down working under Pete's dodgy car, when I heard this motorbike pull up. It was the bike I first noticed, it was an old Enfield, you don't see many of those round here. The chap took off his helmet, spoke all posh like, and said there was something wrong with his bike, probably the petrol mix. I was a bit puzzled, because there was nothing wrong with the sound of the bike at all, but I dutifully said I would look at it, so I bent down and twizzled with a few bits and pieces, but like I said it was fine. He then said he was looking for this girl, she was a runaway and her parents were dead worried about her. He whipped out this photograph. It was a girl in her school uniform, she had a big hat on, no make-up, it was definitely Ruby about three years younger, it was difficult to tell with the hat. But there was the same dark hair alright. He said there was fifty pounds in it for me, if I could tell him where she was, or where I had seen her. I just kept working slowly and methodically on the bike. I said I hadn't seen anyone like that. I kept my head down so he couldn't see my eyes, and kept my hands real steady." Dave had always been good in a crisis. He had got two children out of a car when it skidded on ice and was half way hanging out over the gorge above the river two winter's back. "He asked me did I live in the village, and did I know everyone there, I said I did. I told him his bike was fine. I wouldn't accept any money from him although he offered me a tenner. I don't know but there was something very menacing about that guy. Cold, calculating," Dave shivered. "It was really belting down by rain by then, and quite dark, so the guy just put his helmet on again, circled his motorbike around and headed back to the New Town. I reckon we were lucky the weather was so horrendous, otherwise he might have been tempted to hang around longer and have more of a look. I waited till he had gone down past the bend. Then I made my way across the road, and over some of the shop back gardens and yards so he couldn't track me. I came straight to Owain's, I knew he had a shotgun, and we came straight up here. I'm sorry

I didn't call you Evan, but I didn't want you leading him to Ruby."

"You did a marvellous job, thanks mate, thanks so much!" Evan clapped Dave on the shoulder. Thank goodness it was Dave Ruby's father had talked to.

They all stayed in the shepherd's hut for about an hour, Evan changed out of his wet and muddy clothes. Goodness knows what he was going to wear to work tomorrow. But Ruby was safe and that was all that mattered. He made everyone a cup of tea.

"Do you think he had an idea that Ruby was here?" Asked Evan.

"No," said Dave, "He was just fishing. Probably looking at all the train and bus links radiating out from Bristol in a grid search, seeing if he can pick up a lead somewhere."

"That would be right," said Ruby. She'd been pretty quiet until now. Evan hugged her tightly.

"Do you think he'll be back?" He asked.

"He might be," said Ruby. "OK, he found nothing at Brynafon this time, but I guess it'll depend if he's got anything that connects me going West."

"I think we were lucky this time," said Dave.

Evan hoped they'd be so lucky in the future. But could they hope to hide Ruby forever? Sooner or later he would find her. "Can't we just go to the police?" he asked forlornly, knowing what the answer would be.

"No," said Ruby firmly. "The minute you make that call and its filed electronically, he'll find it, and me."

Chapter 7

The next visitor to The Hill, was altogether more welcome and far more unexpected.

The week had begun slowly enough. Evan was still on edge about Ruby's father. Ruby, on the other hand, although quieter than normal, had taken it more in her stride. The shotgun was hidden under a rug. Evan would have to fit a locked cabinet for it. Ruby was sitting on the bed that morning swinging her long pale legs, with a frown on her face.

"Are you thinking about your Dad's visit?" Evan asked as her brushed his teeth, he was going to walk Ruby down to the bakery every morning from now on.

"No," said Ruby, "the bakery."

Ruby had been made assistant manager of the bakery, meaning in fact manger, as Gwyneth, the elderly lady who owned it and lived upstairs, was a sleeping partner in more ways than one. The bakery staff checked on her three times a day, her mind was all there, but her body was now very frail.

"It's the price of the bread the suppliers sell us, it's going up again. I don't know how people will afford it, and it's not even good stuff, not filling and nutritious. Tasteless too. We have no control over it, it all sent up from The New Town." Ruby was still frowning. Her legs kicked the bed more vigorously in her agitation.

Evan smiled, Ruby could be the only person who'd just had her life threatened and was thinking about other people. He smiled again and took hold of her hand and kissed her. That's one of the many things he loved about Ruby.

"Bread used to be made on site, there's still the old oven and chimney there. Do you think you could have a look at it, see if we could get it to function again, seeing you made the wood burning stove here? We'd need a baker and flour supplier of course." Stated Ruby.

It was Evan's turn to frown. "Gosh, I'm not sure I'm up to safety testing a bread oven, but tell you what I'll get Dave to have a look at it with me as he's an engineer, but I think I might be able to help with a baker. I went to school with Rhys, he now works at the bread factory in New Town, I am sure he'd be interested, I'll give him a call when I get to the office."

Ruby smiled, "What would I do without you?" She laughed kissing him.

Ruby finished drinking her tea and tidying her hair. Evan noticed that she had pulled back her fringe and clipped it over her head, her hair had grown longer too. Gone was the Cleopatra bob. It suited her; Ruby's fine chiselled features looked good however her hair was. Ruby noticed him looking at her.

"I think, the less that I look like that photo that my Dad has of me, the better." Commented Ruby.

Evan, Dave and Rhys gathered at the bakery after it had closed at 5pm. Evan's mum was there too, she had been offered Ruby's assistant manager's position, but had not wanted to take on the extra days and responsibilities of the job, she was quite content with her part time job. Mary, the pastor's wife had just joined the staff, a homely, sensible lady, who spoke both English and Welsh, she was a God send in many ways. The former assistant manager Dyllis had retired, and with Ruby's promotion, a replacement was required. Mary was a plump, motherly lady who everyone in the village respected and knew. The Pastor had not been keen for his wife to work. But Mary had been a shop girl before she was married, and was keen to have a life of her own, and not just be the Pastor's wife, and as she argued most succinctly to her husband. What better way was there to spread God's word and love and the work of the chapel, than to get out there and engage with all the young mums and elderly people who came and had a tea and coffee, or bought their bread at the bakery? Besides it was only a few mornings a week.

So, there they were, all standing round the small space that had been the bakery kitchen. Dave and Evan were on the floor on their backs, looking up the chimney, Dave had brought some cleaning rods, Rhys was studying the walls of the bake oven for cracks, and then went outside to check the chimney.

"It'll need a good clean, and I'll give it a trial run, but I think with a bit of repointing it'll be good, it wasn't that long since it was used really." Said Rhys.

"It was used till 1980," said Evan's mother.

"That's right," said Mary. "The smells coming out of here were heavenly!"

"I'd like the job," said Rhys, "I hate that factory in the New Town, I've wanted to make really good artisan bread and cakes for years now. I'll have a word with the heritage mill over in the next valley, and see if they can supply us with the flour. It's lovely flour they grind there, all grown locally, and they can't shift the stuff, not enough tourists to buy it, you see."

"I'll have to OK it with Gwyneth, the bakery owner," stated Ruby, "I had a word with her this morning, and said I'd tell her the outcome. Mind you, you'd have to make a profit sharpish. We're only just breaking even, if it doesn't pay there's no wages, are we all agreed?"

The women nodded.

"Let's see what Gwyneth has to say then!" Said Ruby.

It was inadvertently what caused Gwyneth's accident. Gwyneth came downstairs to see the state of the old bake oven herself early the next morning. Ruby found her lying in her nightdress at the bottom of the stairs. She comforted the old lady as best she could, laying her coat over her and telephoned for an ambulance, poor Gwyneth was in a lot of pain, with what looked like a broken hip, fortunately she had only been there for five minutes, the poor old lady was crying loudly. Evan's mother fetched blankets and a pillow from upstairs, to make her more comfortable, and Mary held her hand and talked to her and said a prayer for her.

Mercifully the ambulance from the New Town was quick to arrive that time in the morning and half an hour later, kind paramedics were loading her into the vehicle. Evan's mother had packed a suitcase of clothes for her, and Mary was going to go with her. People were kind like that when there was a crisis in Brynafon. Gwyneth managed to utter into Ruby's ear before the paramedics took her away.

"Get that bread oven going again, I'd like that."

Ruby had her go ahead, although not in the circumstances intended.

That evening Ruby was again digging test pits on The Hill. This time the three middle ones. The earth here was two to three inches deep, although the far pit only went down an inch because it hit a rocky outcrop, so the work was not arduous. Evan learnt, as he stood by her and helped her, that it wasn't at all the same as digging a hole for a fence post. One didn't just dig deeply and shovel the soil out; no this was very precise and meticulous. The hole had to be recorded exactly, where it was on the plan, and what finds, if any were made. After measuring out where it should be, a square foot was dug. The sides had to be dead vertical, and not slope and be tidy. The soil was then taken off in a layer an inch at a time, using a brick layer's trowel, which Evan had purchased for her. The soil was then sieved, using his mother's garden sieve. The soil was carefully examined at every stage for any artefact. The hole was then photographed, and any finds with a ruler against it, so the size of the artefact could be recorded in the photograph.

The first hole produced a bit of a sheared off bolt from a farm implement. Several chickens jumped into the hole and started scraping around, Ruby had to shoo them off, and a sheep butted her on the behind and she lurched forward into the hole. Evan could not help giggling, he tried to supress it with a little cough.

"I never had this mentioned on my degree course or field work. The hazards of field archaeology!" She laughed. "Good job, there is nothing of value in this test pit, otherwise my foot would have squashed it!" The hole was photographed, and then filled in again, so no sheep, or themselves could fall into it. Evan was in charge of sieving and putting the earth back. The far side test pit revealed nothing. The one to the right of the dip under the nose did however. Evan was in charge of digging this one under Ruby's watchful supervision. He was praised for taking it nice and slowly, and being neat and methodical. All things Evan was good at. Two inches down, Evan came across a gold pin about an inch long. The sharp end was now blunt, and it was slightly bowed. It had a little gold ball on the end, the whole pin was only an inch long.

"Wow," said Evan, "a find, you do know what you are doing."

Ruby handled it carefully. "So, we can say artefacts are definitely occurring below the nose of The Hill, but not above it, and from where it was positioned, likely from The Hill itself."

"My Hill, contains gold and artefacts?" Asked Evan.

"It's looking that way," stated Ruby. She washed off and photographed the pin placing it on a piece of white paper with the ruler beside it, and recorded it on the site map. "It'll be interesting to see what is in the bottom test pits when we come to dig them. ...Also, have you noticed, there is a pattern emerging?"

It had not occurred to Evan to notice, or even look for a pattern.

"Yes, "Said Ruby. "Not only are most of the finds Saxon, with this one it is difficult to say, but they are all the size of a two pound coin or less, which means the conduit that they are being deposited here through, must be very small, not bigger than a two pound coin at one point anyway."

"Gosh," said Evan, "You're right, no wonder we haven't found it, it could be under any piece of grass or stone." They had been searching for some time for a hole in The Hill particularly by the nose.

"Can't wait to dig the last test pits, but it's getting dark. I put on a moussaka; it should be ready now." Happily, she led him hand in hand off the Hill, Evan was convinced she was trying to skip in the large wellingtons!

Evan was glad there were a few things planned this week to take their minds off Ruby's father's visit. On Saturday evening Jed and Nick had invited them and Owain to Manor Farm for a meal. They bundled in to the Land Rover. Owain was keen to see inside Manor Farm, he said he had not been there for a good fifty years.

It was a lovely heart-warming occasion, wine, beer and talked flowed. Nick had cooked a goose from one of the local farms. He was obviously the cook, as well as the chauffeur and all his other jobs. He said he'd had a stint as a chef in a hotel in Yorkshire between riding accidents. Molly the cat had the left overs and looked happy and content laid out in front of the fire. Nick was asking Owain about his sheep dog.

"What you be wanting one of those for, you've not got any sheep at the moment Nick?"

"For rounding up the Old Bugger," laughed Nick. "I don't know if it's the drink or drugs that got to him, or if it's dementia setting in, mind you he was always dead scatty. But he goes for these walks to clear his mind for writing songs, and he's never back in time for dinner. Sometimes I have to go out and look for him, and sometimes he's gone and got lost!"

"It's true enough," Agreed Jed. "Nick's right cross when I spoil one of lovely meals, and so he should be. I just seem to lose it all when I'm out in the hills. Mind you, since I've come here the writing's come back, I was all dried up in London but now they just seem to be pouring through me, I call them my little gifts from heaven!"

"Tell them your good news, go on!" Said Nick.

"Yeah," replied Jed, "I knew there was something I wanted to tell you. Well my record company usually takes a couple of my songs every so often, but this month they've taken three and want two more."

"Wow," said Ruby, "That's great."

"It's what keeps us going, Jed's writing," Stated Nick.

"Yeah, I split the money I get in two and Nick has half, although he should by rights have more because he does more than his fair share of work here, any over goes to do up this old heap a bit."

It was clear Jed and Nick had a good old working friendship.

"Furthermore," said Jed. "They want me to do another album, me at my age after all this time, I never thought it! Apparently, I still have a bit of a cult following. Of course, my music's quite different to what it was then. That's where you come in Ruby."

"Me!" Said Ruby astounded.

"Yeah, there's two violins in quite a few of my more ballad type pieces, so Nick tracked down old Benedict, our public-school boy violinist, he's now retired of course from the Philharmonic. I'll do the guitar and key boards, we'll get a bass in, another guitarist and a drummer, they'll be just session musicians of course, and we'll record it here, I've got the equipment, and Nick can manage all that stuff."

"I'm amazed," said Ruby slightly breathless. "I've never played in anything professionally before, I knew our little jamming sessions were going well, but I never imagined this!"

"And I want you on the front cover, with that violin of yours in that red dress, I'll do the photography myself against the stone work of the barn. I'll be on the back cover; they've got to have my ugly old mug on it apparently. Got to think of a new band name, some derivation on rainbows."

Ruby just hoped her Dad wasn't a Roaring Rainbows fan, and didn't see her on the new album. No, he was more Wagner. But she looked different now anyhow, and Dad or no Dad she wasn't going to let anything spoil this opportunity. She just wished she could share it with her old friends at University.

"I'll let you know when it all kicks off, another glass of red wine Ruby, and coke for you Evan? Owain had dozed off in his chair some time ago.

"I think I will," said Ruby.

The next day they were invited to Bill Clackett's and his family for Sunday lunch. They slept in until after 10a.m. when there was a quick rush to let the indignant hens out, before Evan jumped on Ruby on her way back inside.

"Give a girl a chance!" She said with a laugh. Clasping her hands round his neck as he carried her back to bed. It was another hour before they emerged again.

"We better get ready," said Evan somewhat reluctantly. "Don't want to be late for Bill and Margaret!"

Margaret was Bill's second wife, the first having left him for a flash Harry of an Estate Agent in Swindon. After that Bill had had the opportunity to buy the New Town Estate Agency, which he had seen advertised in a trade journal. It was just what he needed to get away from Swindon, and the taunts of his neighbours and other Estate Agents. Not that they were all unsympathetic. The long hours and weekends worked in Estate Agency were known to be a killer to all but the most robust marriages. Bill had met Margaret, a local girl when she had temped for a him a couple of years after he came to the New Town. By that time, he had built up a thriving business, and was feeling a lot more confident about life he general. He liked the New Town, it had the feeling of an up and coming place, there were all the facilities he was used to, Bill was not a country boy, and there was a good river to fish in, Bill liked fishing. Margaret was the daughter of a local clergyman, a homely girl, who was happy where she was, she had lots of friends, a good supportive family and just wanted a family of her own. She'd had brown wavy shoulder length hair, rosy cheeks, a lovely warm smile, and warm blue eyes with a warm caring nature to match. This time round Bill had thought with his head not just his heart and organ. Long legs, a very short skirt, a toothy smile, dyed blonde hair and lots of too orange makeup, weren't for him again.

Bill and Margaret had been very happy together. They had a nice thirties detached house in the best suburbs of the New Town, a nice garden with roses, a small terrier named Bert, and two children, a girl and a boy, Ann and James who had come back from their prospective universities this weekend. Ann was studying law, in her last year and James was in his second year of accountancy. They were a thoroughly nice family, and Evan was keen to see them all, and introduce Ruby.

Ruby had other advantages he discovered, other than her obvious charms. He had suddenly become socially acceptable with her, there was another Sunday lunch planned in a few weeks' time at the Pastor's and his wife Mary's. He was no longer the single guy, the loner. Not that he had ever been the type of guy who liked to be single, play the field and have a stream of ladies. One girl at a time was enough for him, and if he was without one for a bit, it didn't bother him. He didn't have to have a girl at his side, on his beck and call to give him status. He had enough independence of character. However, with Ruby at his side, life had improved in nearly every way. She was very socially acceptable and astute. She was charming, a good conversationalist, witty, and had a genuine interest in people – and she always looked stunning. He was very lucky indeed, he thought to himself.

Not that she'd looked stunning coming down in the Land Rover. She had again slumped in her seat, his large hoodie on, hood up over her head. They had called into the department store where Evan had seen a dress in the window, a classic floral 1950s style that Evan thought she would look smashing in, she needed a new dress for the summer, and he wanted to buy it for her. She had already been asked to a couple of baptisms by the young mums in the village, and she needed something appropriate to wear. Ruby purchased a pair of white high heeled shoes and a pair of flat strappy sparkly sandals to go with the dress and a pale lemon cardigan. Evan smiled at her when she trotted out of the changing room in them. She was his girl. Ruby kept on the dress and cardigan to visit Bill's, although the hoodie had to go over the top until the last minute.

Ruby liked the Clackett family as much as they liked her. Margaret showed her the garden, she played with Bert the dog with his pully toy, and she chatted to Ann and James about their University courses and was generally a success all round.

"This one's a keeper, don't be too long in popping the question lad," Bill whispered to him under his breath on their way into the dining room.

"Soon," said Evan, "very soon," he had been making plans in that direction.

The table was beautifully laid with flowers, silver table wear, napkins and silver candle sticks. Margaret like to do things properly. The meal was the real deal as well, a lovely roast lamb with rosemary, gravy, potatoes, a selection of veg, including some lovely fresh asparagus, and a huge apple pie for dessert, with apples that had been stored from the tree in their garden. Evan didn't think he'd ever been as full. Yes, he wanted this for his Ruby, a nice house with a garden, a family and a dog, if she wanted that too. Perhaps she wanted to be out in Egypt digging? He fervently hoped not.

It seemed as if he couldn't have been happier – when Bill landed the bombshell – he was retiring, and he was selling the Estate Agency. Evan knew he was due to retire; he had worked longer than he needed to set enough money aside to get his children through the costly process of university. Now it appeared, with the development at Brynafon, Manor Farm and the development by the railway at the New Town, Bill calculated he would be able to retire at the end of September.

Evan knew Bill had wanted to retire for some time, but it still came as a shock, he sat there speechless for a few moments, it was Ruby who politely filled the gap, saying how hard she knew he had worked, before Evan was finally able to say.:

"I'll miss you Bill."

There was an inkling of good news on the horizon though. Dodgy Dick, the other Estate Agent in town was no longer trading. His premises were abandoned and post was piling up on the doorstep.

"Disappeared on Wednesday morning, rumour has it that he hadn't paid his tax bill and creditors and a loan shark were after him, hasn't been seen in or about New Town since!"

Evan managed to raise a smile, so Bill had no competition this Spring and probably Summer.

"I've had four of Dodgy Dick's clients come to me already." Said Bill, helping himself to a second helping of the apple pie. "Of course, you'll have first refusal Evan to buy the New Town shop," he nodded to Evan. "The Brynafon one I'll sell, but not as a going concern, it's not been making a profit for some time now."

It made sense, Evan thought, Brynafon didn't need an estate agents, it needed more shops, a chemist and a post office again.

"I've decided you'll have half of the profits from the Brynafon and Manor Farm developments, it'll give you a bit of a nest egg to start up with." Said Bill.

Evan knew it was a most generous gift from Bill.

"Thank you," he said meekly.

"How's the Manor Farm developments going?" Asked Bill.

"The two rentals should occupy next week, Claire and Bronwyn are taking one unit for their horse trekking business, and the stables and adjoining fields, and the holiday let should be up and running next week, too. I have a couple of ladies who want to book it as soon as it's ready. All the utilities were in, we just needed the places updated as they were the former head grooms and the game keepers' cottages. The sewerage feed to the tank has now been completed and they are newly painted and refurbished. The other units need a complete over haul for the two families who will be leasing them jointly, I'd say mid-summer for them."

"Splendid," said Bill, "and planning permission has gone through for the houses at Brynafon opposite the school, and the big development here in the New Town by the railway. I hope work will start on those next week and they'll be completed by the end of the Summer."

Evan and Ruby thanked their hosts for their hospitality, but both were quiet on the way home. Evan would be out of a job, unless he could afford to buy the estate agency in the New Town, which he wasn't sure he wanted or could afford. He liked it where he was, going out and about to the farms and rented hill side cottages, not being tied to a desk all day in the industrialisation of New Town. He so wanted to ask Ruby to marry him, but now he had nothing to offer her. Finding work locally was hard, and he'd always had a job straight from school, and cash in his pocket, but not now, not soon. He could not ask a girl to marry him if he did not have the means to support her and a family. He was old fashioned like that, he had always had it drilled in to him by his parents and the Pastor, that if you wanted a wife, you made sure you could adequately provide for her.

Ruby took his hand tightly as if she knew what he was thinking.

"Did you always want to be an estate agent?" She asked.

"God, no," said Evan. "I just literally walked into it, and found I was good at it. It was just there, this notice in the window as I left school on my last day, on my way to the bus stop for home. I just walked in, talked to Bill, and he offered me the job straight away. The next day I started work." He sighed. "It's not so easy nowadays, no jobs, no prospects. I don't know what I'll do. I don't really want to work in the New Town, I'd like to stay in Brynafon."

Evan frowned, his options seemed limited. How could he possibly propose to Ruby now? He had nothing to offer her. That was what he thought, hurt the most.

Ruby squeezed his hand again. "We'll think of something for you," she said. "My final exams are next month, then I'll be free to work more." Ruby paused for a minute or two. "I love you Evan, that's what matters to me," said Ruby kissing him on the cheek.

Evan's heart jumped. Those were the words he wanted to hear more than any others.

"I can shear sheep," said Evan suddenly.

"Well then," said Ruby, "so you have got some skills then! Not just in the bedroom!"

Chapter 8

It was the next Sunday that the surprise visitor turned up. It was very early in the morning and Evan was up letting their new chickens that were now housed just down from the shepherd's hut in a splendid new coop Evan had made them out of pallets. Ruby just adored them, fluffy balls of yellow feathers, with their mother a large ginger bird. Evan undid the coop door and they toddled out happily to greet the dawn.

He turned, sensing, rather than seeing a movement on the Hill. Through the mist he could just see a rotund figure emerging. He froze, was it Ruby's Dad back? It looked too short and rotund, but he could not be certain, he quickly made his way to the door of the shepherd's hut, he opened the door a fraction, Ruby was still inside getting dressed.

"Ssh, say inside, there's someone on The Hill." He whispered.

He strained his eyes into the swirling mist. The strange figure was making its way cautiously down the mountain from the direction of Spring Farm, which was high above the top of The Hill. A track, used occasionally by hikers came from there, down across the top of The

Hill to come out to where the terraced houses finished and the track to Manor Farm started.

He squinted, into the hazy sun rising in the east, making the fog opaquer. The figure did seem to be on that track, and it was far too small for Ruby's Dad, it was more like a figure of a child. It was definitely on the portly side; the impression wasn't helped by a rucksack on the back.

Most probably a hiker, but on their own at this time of the morning? He or she must have come over the mountain in the dark, it was awfully dangerous. They must be lost. They couldn't have come from the rental cottage at Spring Farm because Bill Clackett's Estate Agency handled the bookings for it, and he knew it was unbooked. It had yet to have a booking this season.

The figure wore a bobble hat in a bright colour, and had a scarf muffled over his or her face.

They had one of those very old yellow waterproofs on, with a very sturdy pair of old leather hiking boots, and it looked like close-fitting horse-riding breeches, shooting breeches or leggings on in an indeterminate colour. There was a stick in the left hand that acted as a walking pole. The figure was still coming, it paused at the top of The Hill for a minute looked around, and back the way it had just come from, it then made its way carefully down the side of The Hill. Evan could tell by the movement the figure was not young, but was not old either. A hand went out to stroke a sheep that came to investigate. The figure had now turned and was coming towards him and the shepherd's hut.

"Ruby," he whispered, "Get the gun, it's not your Dad, but I don't know who it is."

He heard the gun barrel slam closed behind the door.

The figure came steadily and directly up to him, there was a smile, a thatch of a blond bob sticking out under the hat, and blue, blue eyes behind glasses.

A purple woolly gloved had shot out.

"I'm Dr. Elizabeth Mary Forster of Bristol University Archaeology department, and you young man must be the young gentleman that Ruby talks about so fondly!"

"Good God!" Said Evan, absolutely staggered, his mouth gaped uncouthly open. "Pleased to meet you," he added suddenly recognising the face from the cover of Ruby's archaeology book. Recovering his posture, he proffering his hand too. "How on earth did you find us!"

"Ruby!" Called Evan, "It's your professor, put the gun down. ...You weren't followed, were you?" he asked peering over her shoulders into the gloom.

"No, absolutely not, I took care, that's why I hiked in over the mountains in the dark." Said Dr. Forster.

"Wow, do you know how treacherous that is?" asked Evan.

Dr. Forster was truly a remarkable lady.

Ruby threw her arms around Dr.Forster and they both gave each other a warm embrace. Evan put on a warming pot of tea, Dr.Forster was quite cold, the fact that she had survived at all was remarkable, let alone found them.

"How did you find us, I thought we had been extra careful?" Said Ruby, a little worried. Dr.Forster sat in a relaxed fashion on the bed with her mauve mohair mittens cradling the hot tea, looking like she had lived in a shepherd's hut all her life. She glanced round.

"Nice place," she said, "I wish I'd had one of these when I was a youngster on digs years ago."

Evan decided he better put on some more porridge for her, she clearly had not had breakfast.

"Well, remember I am a Landscape Archaeologist, so I am an expert in reading and interpreting maps and landscapes. You loosely described in your email what The Hill was like, that it was by a river that ran north south, and a settlement. The dimensions of The Hill you described made this the most likely place. I did take me a few weeks scouring all the maps of the Wales to find it, but I was pretty certain I had the right place."

Dr. Forster gratefully took the steaming bowl of porridge Evan had prepared for her.

"Wonderful," she said. "Thank you so much, delicious!" Evan had added honey to it to give her back some energy. "Well, as luck would happen the history department was looking at an old priory in the next valley and a few other things around the area, and they had a last-minute vacancy on the field trip, so I filled the place! I said I was hoping to retire some time somewhere in Wales and was looking at areas, they quite believed me. So, I set my post-grad student my classes for a few days and here I am. I walked out of the camp last evening, I could see from the priory there was an old drovers route running, west east, so I followed that all the way. Our modern roads tend to run north south, but old prehistoric tracks run east west, like the Ridgeway. That was one of the things that interested me about your Hill, it wasn't just on the north south river, but it is actually just off this small forgotten east west track way. Having come over that track, I believe it is very, very old indeed, prehistoric in fact. If you wanted to get goods to and from the west coast of Wales, you'd travel this way, then you could intersect with the river to take them north or cross over to England."

Dr. Forster took a few more spoonfuls of her porridge. "That's better," she said. "Well, I started off Saturday night in the late afternoon. When it got really dark, I bivouacked just under the top of The Hill in an old sheep fold, then as soon as it started to lighten I came over the summit and made my way down here. It wasn't meant to be so misty, but the mist did a great job at covering me. I know I wasn't followed, I kept looking back, and I walked at night without my head torch." She paused. "I've said I'll be back Wednesday; I hope that is alright with you? I just couldn't resist seeing my star student, and what you're up to here, exciting isn't it!"

Clearly Dr. Elizabeth Mary Forster was an amazing woman, thought Evan again.

"I'll take you back as far as Spring Farm on Wednesday in the Land Rover," said Evan hastily, not wanting Dr. Forster to repeat such a hazardous journey. If he could manage the time, he'd walk her most of the way down to the priory and then hike back up to the farm.

Evan left Ruby and Dr. Forster to catch up while he continued with some of his morning chores with the sheep. By the time he came back in Dr.Forster had clearly de-thawed and her coat, gloves and bobble hat had come off. Ruby was showing Dr. Forster the chart on the wall, when Evan re-entered the shepherd's hut. Ruby excitedly asked him to show her the finds from The Hill. Dr. Forster studied each one with great care, whipping a little magnifying glass out of her pocket. She nodded, and cooed.

"Yes, "she said handling each one gently. "It is what I thought, a cluster of Saxon finds, but a back ground scattering of Neolithic and earlier, showing there has been some activity or trade through Brynafon for a very long time. Can I help you dig the rest of the test pits?"

She asked.

Evan nodded. He couldn't believe two people were actually interested in his Hill!

"I'll see if there's a room going for you at the Dragon and Dagger pub, if that's alright?" said Evan.

Dr. Forster nodded her approval. "I thought I'd see that Saxon dagger that was found here on Monday, I believe it is in the New Town museum?" Said Dr. Forster. "Is there a bus there?"

Evan told her the bus times, and said he would show her where he and Ruby worked and she could pop in any time she needed anything. She also needed to be introduced to Owain. She nodded approval.

The foggy day had brightened to one of those glorious sunny Spring days, and after Dr. Forster had rested and they had a round of croissants and coffee, she expressed an interest in seeing the river and the surrounding area. She was particularly interested in the path down to the crossing point at the river, and to discover if there were the remnants of a path up the opposite side of the bank.

Evan borrowed a small blow up dingy from his friend Pete, which he loaded into his rucksack while Ruby rustled up a ham and cheese picnic, which Dr. Forster placed into her rucksack, Ruby carried the oars and they set off down the track opposite Owain's house at beginning of the terrace houses down to the river.

Dr. Forster paused looking back at the road they had just crossed, musing:

"I think that drovers track would have come over the mountains and down beside the nose of the Hill, through Owain's farmyard and the village square then across the modern road and then headed down here. The present track only diverts to meet up with the Manor Farm track where it does, because the terrace houses have now been built. The track definitely has the look of a prehistoric long-distance route about it. Have you noticed those couple of stones at various points, I think they are way markers."

Evan was pleased he had noticed them, but had just thought of them as random upright stones. But it made sense, particularly if there was snow covering the ground and the track, you could look from one stone to another he suddenly realised.

Evan had never thought about linking up the tracks, he was beginning to see his local landscape in a whole new way, as a series of layers of history, like an onion skin, not just the landscape that he saw before his eyes.

Dr. Forster was interested in the track down, it was steep, but Evan knew that sheep had been transported down that way.

"It probably would have been a bit wider and have zigzagged down more than it does now. You can see where rock fall when it is wet has caused little landslides here and there."

Evan looked around where she pointed. It was amazing what you could see when you looked around, and knew what to look for. Dr. Forster took her time, she didn't just hike down to the bottom as he and Ruby had done, she stopped frequently, paused and looked around.

"Look, there," she said pointing to a slight terracing in the steep valley side about twelve feet from them.

"That's where the track went, but you can see above it, it was cut off by a rock fall, so the track now diverts over here to the right a bit. You can see there that it was wider too." Evan was amazed Dr. Forster could see so much, she didn't just look at something like him, she interpreted it in the landscape, looking for clues in the past coming down time as remnants now in the present.

The day was truly beautiful, they had their coats off now, mist was rising eerily from the river, and thin wisps danced off the trees and vegetation around them as the day heated up. The trees bowed down to reach the water here and a king fisher suddenly darted on the opposite bank.

"It's stunning here." Said Dr. Forster. "I can see why you like it Ruby."

Dr. Forster took off her boots and socks and dipped her feet in the chilly water.

"That's better, my feet have done a bit of travelling these past few days, both they and my boots have seen better days!"

Evan smiled. Dr. Forster had a keen sense of fun, and a real zeal for life. Evan could see why Ruby thought so much of her. Six months ago, he thought, I didn't know Ruby and I didn't know Dr. Forster, I was the odd guy in the shiny suit with an obsession for The Hill. How life had changed!

Ruby unpacked the picnic. "A bottle of red wine! Thanks Evan." Evan had hidden it in his rucksack for the women, he brought it out with a flourish.

"Just don't you two drink all of it, I'm not carrying you both back up!" Evan laughed.

Ruby handed the bread, cheese and ham round. She explained to Dr. Forster their plans for the bakery, and how the café had become a real hub of the community, and slowly the sleepy village was coming to life.

"Well," said Dr. Forster. "When you've finished your degree, you can work on your masters and PHD, you would have to travel around of course, but Brynafon would be as good a base as any. The Welsh Universities are very good, and you're really not so far from Bristol, if you wanted to get some work with one of them. I'll have a look at the work you've done so far, and give you some pointers for the exams."

Ruby thanked her.

Dr. Forster was looking across the river. A kingfisher was obliging perching on a tree branch over hanging the river near where the track upwards should start. "I can't see a track on the other side, but the remains of one will be there somewhere under the trees. Have you looked on that side yet Ruby?"

Ruby shook her head.

"Well we need to," continued Dr. Forster. You need to find that track, and you need to see if there is anything else like The Hill on the other side."

"You think there might be another Hill?" Asked Evan surprised.

"It depends what it is, a small fortification, may have something like that on the other side of the river, if it is some type of burial mound, which I think is the more likely due to the nature of the finds, it probably doesn't have a twin on the other side."

It took Evan a good half hour to inflate the little boat, there was only room for him and Ruby. Dr. Forster was quite pleased to lay resting on this side of the river. Evan took the rope he had been carrying and tied it to a stout tree, he wasn't going to take the chance of the boat drifting far down stream, if they got into difficulties Dr. Forster could haul them back. Ruby put the oars together, and with giggles, wobbles and splashing they lowered themselves carefully in and Evan rowed powerfully to the other side. They found what looked like a landing place, coming down at an angle to the water, Evan rowed strongly back up a little as Ruby hauled on the trees. Boat safely pulled up they looked around. Evan had also brought a scythe; it came in handy in cutting back the under growth. It was hard work; this side was steeper and more densely covered in woods. Sometimes they followed the track that was more of a goat's track, sometimes they lost it completely and sometimes they had to take detours. Fortunately, the unusually warm day meant it was drier than usual, but the humidity was high, and the rock still glistened wet in places. The old track seemed to zig zag more. It took them a good hour to reach the top and the road, where they collapsed in a puffing heap. They drank the rest of the water. Evan was pleased at Ruby's scrambling abilities, it boded well for his surprise trip for her next week.

"You're a good climber, Ruby," he said between puffs.

"Oh, there was a climbing wall at University and I went on a few climbing trips, and I was taking a twice weekly ballet class at my convent school until I finished. Ballet keeps you fit and supple. It's good for an archaeologist to know basic rope work and how to climb, it can come in useful on some more extreme sites."

There was so much he didn't know about Ruby still, he thought. Him, he was simple, a boy with an obsession, not much at school, one job and a few mates, he thought. But Ruby, she was altogether someone far more complex.

"You go that way," Ruby said to Evan pointing north, "for five minutes, I'll take the road south."

Evan nodded.

They both returned back still out of breath.

"Anything?" Asked Ruby.

"I couldn't see anything that looked like any type of mound or hill, it was all flat and wooded either side of the road."

"Same here, there was nothing showing on the OS map, I checked before we left, but a small mound would not have shown up. No there's definitely no hill forts, and it doesn't look like there are any burial mounds either. Often you get a clump of Bronze Age ones together."

They made their way carefully down the steep hillside, and back to the boat.

"Nothing," said Ruby, as she reported back to Dr. Forster when they reached the other side. Dr. Forster had been sound asleep on a picnic blanket on the rock. It was amazing she could sleep soundly on the hard flat rock, and quite a relief she hadn't rolled over and fallen in the river, thought Evan.

"As I suspected," she said. "So, your Hill is a one-off feature in these parts, making it less like a fortification, when I would expect an opposing one on the English bank, and more like some sort of burial mound."

The walk up the steep path back to the village was slow. It had become very muggy and a bit thundery. Dr. Forster paused half way up to catch her breath. Evan was glad of the break, the wet blow up dingy was twice the weight it had been on the way down.

Dr. Forster looked at him appreciatively. "I could do with a strong chap like you on my digs!" She said.

"It comes with hauling sheep around since eight years old!" smiled Evan.

There were just a few heavy ominous rain drops falling by the time they reached the top. Evan took Dr. Forster to the Dragon and Dagger to check in. Ruby took the first shower in the converted cupboard in the Estate Agency while Evan fetched Dr. Forster's belongings which she had left in a plastic bag in the shepherd's hut.

It was raining hard by the time they dined at the Dragon and Dagger that evening. Talk soon came around to Ruby's father.

"It can't go on like this," stated Dr. Forster, "that man wrecking your life, Ruby." She frowned. "What to do though? That's the question. The main thing is for now to keep yourself safe, dear. I must admit you couldn't have chosen a better hide out than Brynafon, no mobile phone signal, no CCTV cameras, not on a through route anywhere, no passing trade. It limits the people going in and out through the place and seeing you."

Ruby had told Dr. Forster about her father's tentative visit to Brynafon.

"Fortunately, he's not visited again," said Ruby, between mouthfuls of lamb.

"Ah, well I think I may have had a hand it that... he's probably in York," smiled Dr. Forster.

"York? How's that?" Ruby looked at Dr. Forster with large eyes.

"Well he'd been seen hanging round the University gates for a week after you disappeared, Ruby. He'd obviously hacked into the University database, as he was looking at photos on his phone then looking at various students. I found out he questioned two of your class mates. That boy, Chris, who's hardly ever at class, and wouldn't know what time of day it is with the amount of drugs he uses. Chris couldn't remember you at all, and had no idea you were in his class, let alone missing. It must of actually have been one of his few visits to class this year. Then he questioned Hannah, but of course she didn't know anything, just said no one had seen you. Well, I reported him to security, some pervert hassling students at the gate, and he didn't reappear.

Then last week Louise left her smart phone on the desk at the end of class, she's always forgetting something, it was under a piece of paper she'd also left. It was switched on and unlocked. I'm afraid I accessed her Facebook page, and wrote in that she had thought she'd seen you at York station. After all its miles away from here in the wrong direction, goes to lots of places up north and to London, and York has a university course in archaeology, so I thought it was a rather good choice." Dr. Forster looked pleased.

Evan laughed.

"Of course, it won't hold him off for ever, but when you said about him monitoring electronic comm-unications, I thought, why not use that against him?" Ruby's dad had clearly met his match in Dr. Forster.

After the meal conversation went on to more pleasant topics. Dr. Forster said how she had never married, "always married to archaeology, it's no fun for children and babies to be carted round one muddy, cold and rain swept dig after another. The digs are often on moors or inhospitable places because settlements have not been developed there and destroyed the archaeology. But I've been to many interesting sites all over the world, and particularly here in Britain, and met many inspirational people. Now, I am quite happy helping the next generation discover archaeology."

After the meal Pete, Sian and Dave joined them for a drink. Dr. Forster was obviously happy around younger people. She laughed and joked and was the life and soul of the party.

"I'm glad you have so many friends here," she said to Ruby, "and particularly that young man of yours. A strong and kind guy like that can be hard to find."

Ruby smiled quietly to herself. She knew it!

On Monday, after a late start Dr. Forster took herself off to the museum at New Town to see the famous Brynafon Saxon dagger, topped with a piece of amber and decorated with rubies and ornate gold swirls.

That evening Evan, Ruby and Dr. Forster set about the task of digging the remaining three test pits at the bottom of The Hill by the fence line. Here the soil was up to a foot deep. Evan was given his own test pit to dig on the far side, Ruby had the one nearest Owain's farm house, and Dr. Forster took the middle one.

"I seem to be getting more chickens in the hole than anything else!" Ruby laughed, as she extracted yet another ginger fluffy bundle, eager to help her search for worms.

"They'll be home to roost soon." Laughed Evan.

It was Ruby who found the first find, there was another the bit of rusty iron work from a farm implement, then three quarters of the way down, she found two coins. Carefully she washed them off.

Dr. Forster produced her eye glass. "Saxon," she said. "Mercia, shows there was trade between Wales and Mercia. I'll have to look up what these exactly are, I'm not an expert in coins."

Evans pit produced a part of a sheep's jaw, a small piece of Victorian blue and white pottery, and then a small thin piece of flint. He would have missed it entirely, but it was a different shape and texture to the stones and rocks all round it. It was near the bottom of the test pit.

Dr. Forster became very excited. "Probably Mesolithic," she declared, "that's a small arrow head, they weren't barbed yet, that came later, they were like small leaves. See here you can see the manmade cuts as fresh as the day they were made. The tips broken off, so it's been used, impacted with something. That's probably why it was discarded."

Evan handled it carefully and ran his finger along it, it was sharp alright, it could still give a person a nasty cut now.

"Shows there were people moving and hunting through here, since prehistory. We've got no proof of settlement, if they had settled for short times, it would have been on the banks of the river. They'd come by log dugout canoe, and then camped and fished from the shore, and probably hunted in the forest above. Brilliant!" She was in raptures.

But it was the middle pit that was the most interesting. It contained a handle of a Victorian jug, and another piece of blue and white Victorian pottery, but it also contained three further Saxon coins, a bit of twisted gold rope about four inches long, in diameter half the size of Ruby's small finger. Dr. Forster thought might be part of a Saxon torque or bracelet. It was straightish, like a snake with a few slight bends in it. Dr. Forster asked Ruby to lend her her small delicate wrist, she proceeded to carefully bend it round Ruby's wrist.

"That's how it should look, "she said. But the final find was the best of all, it was a small Christian cross about in inch and a half long, beautifully worked and inscribed with Celtic type designs. It was a little twisted, but all the elements of the cross were there. Ruby and Dr. Forster were breathless.

"This is stupendous," said Dr. Forster beaming. "This is Christian, Saxon Christian, so it is likely we are dealing with Christian folk, probably Mercian from across the English border. Possibly a Saxon burial. There just aren't any Saxon burial sites this far West, certainly not in Wales, but possibly they were travelling, either by river or the track and ended up falling on some calamity, which meant one or more people were buried here. Not just anyone either, someone of status, a tribal leader, a very rich trader. This is amazing. You need bring those finds to the museum, Evan."

Evan nodded. He knew it was time he needed to share his Hill, just a little bit.

Chapter 9

The fine weather that had started with Dr. Forster's visit continued throughout her stay. In fact, she seemed to bring the sunshine to Ruby's life in many ways. The women chatted and Evan could see how much Ruby still missed her old life, her university and her friends. But as Ruby said, by the summer she would have finished there anyhow and that life would have gone forever.

That Monday, Dr. Forster visited the New Town museum as discussed seeing the Saxon dagger found at Brynafon for herself. She spent some time talking to the curator, who was delighted to have someone of her calibre and interest visiting the small provincial museum. Dr. Forster brought with her some of Evan's finds, and the new ones that had emerged with the digging of the test pits. She had put it to Evan that when they had the time and the conditions had been dry for some, he should dig a trench linking up the three lower test pits by the hedge line with the houses. This had been agreed by Evan. The curator also agreed to a display cabinet to show off the finds made at The Hill; this would be implemented by the research Ruby was doing into the area. Ruby had already supplied a photograph of The Hill, and a copy of the plan of the finds. The curator, could not believe his luck, nothing this exciting had happened in the three years he'd been there, in fact it had been rather dull for a young man not so long out of his PHD at University, and he had started to apply to move on. But suddenly this looked promising. Dr. Forster promised to keep in touch. It was indeed a happy day for him, and he went back to his lonely, bachelor bed sit with a spring in his step that day, and a determination to visit Evan at the Hill as soon as he had a day off.

That evening Evan, Ruby and Dr. Forster sat out till late on the step of the shepherd's hut with glances of wine and orange juice and chatted. Ruby was telling Dr. Forster about her violin playing for Jed's new album, and how excited she was about it. As darkness fell, they watched the stars, which had so entranced Ruby when she first came to Brynafon, shine brightly in the dark night sky. The wind which had been still all day began to get up, and suddenly The Hill began to sing, a low, wooden flute like moaning, rising and falling with the strength of the wind.

"Extraordinary," exclaimed Dr. Forster. "I've never heard anything like it before." She listened intently.

"You know what this means, Ruby?" She said.

"That there's a hole through The Hill somewhere from west to east, something that artefact up to about an inch and a half can fall through." Said Ruby.

"Not just that!" Dr. Forster almost snapped at Ruby. Evan was quite shocked at her tone, he jolted suddenly, but then with the next sentence, he knew Dr. Forster was challenging Ruby to use and expand that fine mind of hers.

"You're a musician, think! What does it mean, what does the noise, the pitch tell you?"

Ruby listened again.

"Oh, I see!" She said. "How can I have been so stupid! The note is low, like a cello would play, not like a violin. A cello's body is much bigger than a violin's so it produces a lower note. The cavity is much greater. So....it can't just be a narrow tube flowing through The Hill, that would produce a higher note like a flute. No, its low, which means there must be a large cavity in The Hill....a burial chamber probably, not collapsed or filled in! WOW!"

Dr. Forster smiled and put her arm around Ruby. "Precisely," she said. "This is worth excavating with Evan's agreement."

Evan was stunned. He didn't know if he wanted his Hill excavated or not.

"It would mean a shaft, properly supported coming in, probably from the top. It would be a costly and complicated job; structural support would probably be required. The hollow chamber might cave in, it might not, it might be empty, on the other hand from the artefacts we've found so far, it probably contains something, or even someone." Continued Dr. Forster.

Dr. Forster turned to Evan. "These are all things to consider carefully, Evan. What I can do is try to get funding for the excavation, and assemble a provision team together to excavate.

The site would not be revealed, it would be kept strictly under wraps, only I would know where it is, which will keep Ruby quite safe. But secrecy on important digs is paramount anyway, so it would not be considered odd in anyway."

Evan took a big breath, in one way he felt relieved, in another very apprehensive. This was his Hill, it was precious, special.

"Can I think about it?" He asked. He glanced anxiously across at Ruby, would she put pressure on him to the dig the site?

"Of course," said Dr. Forster, "It'll take me time to write a proposal and get funding in place, and even if I get funding, you can always say no, and pull out. The funding will always be used elsewhere. It's your Hill Evan, and your decision."

She paused. "I will warn you that archaeology is destructive, once dug, it can't be undug. It will be partly destroyed or altered. It may completely be destroyed if it collapses. You need to realise that. Of course, we'll use ground penetrating radar to try and see what is there before we even start to dig. If it doesn't look promising it won't happen. The preparatory work is crucial. I suppose Evan, it is up to you to decide, do you want to leave The Hill as it is, with some interesting finds coming out here and there, or do you really want to know what your Hill is? When it was made? Who it was made for? What happened here?"

There were so many questions Evan thought, and he didn't know the answers. He would have a lot to think about that night, and for nights to come. What would Ruby think if he said no? To him that was question number one.

Evan was out and about on Tuesday morning, he took Dr. Forster with him, as he checked on some of the outlying farm cottage rentals, to make sure they were ready for the season. He also checked in on a couple of small farms that were for sale. The weather was beautiful and Dr. Forster enjoyed the views and the countryside at its late Spring best, with lacey cow parsley in the lanes, and the smell and star like flowers of wild garlic under the hedgerows. They visited Manor Farm, the girls with the trekking business were moving in, and Jed had his first booking for the cottage rental. Two elderly ladies with heavy makeup greeted Evan, offering him and Dr. Forster a beer. It wasn't quite what Evan expected for the first rental guests at Manor Farm cottage. They were friendly though.

"Oh, we're Roaring Rainbows fans, we knew this was Jed's place. Been following the Rainbows all our life, and we're just so delighted to be here, and hear that a new album is coming out soon!" Said Sheila. They were like a pair of excited school girls. Sheila had long white hair, and which had once been black, and wore a short mauve mini skirt, and Shirley had brightly dyed red hair and yellow dungarees. Clearly these two still embraced life!

"We've already had our photos taken with Jed in front of his rainbow painted Rolls Royce." Added Shirley enthusiastically. According to Nick, from whom Evan heard later, that wasn't the only activity Jed had undertaken with Sheila and Shirley!

"Had a fine time of it, Jed did, just like the old days." Nick had said with a wink, as he caught up with Evan over a quick drink at the Dragon and Dagger later that week.

Claire and Bronwyn's horses were already munching contentedly in the paddock by the back range of the stable complex. He quickly checked on Claire and Bronwyn, who with the help of their boyfriends were already making good progress.

"We've got booking already for next week trekking, a family of four." Said Claire happily, "so we need to get organised and ready, it's just so nice here, I can't believe how lucky we've been to find this place, our last place was the pits, for us and the horses!"

Evan smiled; he was relieved everyone was happy.

Evan and Dr. Forster had tea at the bakery café around 2pm that day. Ruby was able to take a ten-minute break to join them. The cafe's sun umbrellas were up, and the little village square seemed quite continental with the red geranium handing baskets and horse mangers full of flowers Ruby had put up around the bakery. There was a stall on the side selling homemade local produce, jams, flowers and asparagus from the locals gardens. Evan's mum had made a few cushions to sell, she had been responsible for making the brightly coloured table cloths and the seating cushions, as well as some coloured bunting that fluttered in the slight breeze. The café was full, inside and out, and a few people were sitting on the grass too. There were some hikers, a couple of mountain bikers, a team of four road bikers, a couple of Welsh ponies lashed to railings, dogs running around, chased by a group of toddlers. It had seemed all the world had descended on Brynafon!

"Gosh," said Ruby, "This is the busiest I've known it, and we've nearly run out of bread."

"The café and bakery looks so nice, it's very tempting." commented Dr Forster.

They were joined at their table by Owain, Jed and Nick, and Evan made introductions, before he and Ruby had to get back to work. He left Dr. Forster happily chatting to them.

Dr. Forster was one of those people with the happy capacity to chat with anyone.

That night Ruby cooked a stew with Welsh lamb and fresh wild garlic which they ate out on the steps of the shepherd's hut again. Evan threw one of the woollen Welsh blankets over the women's shoulders. Dr. Forster pulled it to share it over with Evan.

"You don't need to share it!" Laughed Ruby. "He's a tough guy!"

"Talking of guy's" said Dr. Forster. "That Jed is a character, all the things he's done and places he's been, quite a chap!"

If anything, Evan thought, Dr. Forster seemed a little bit smitten!

"I could well get used to it here, when I eventually retire!" Said Dr. Forster. "I thought I would miss the city, but I've so enjoyed walking here, and meeting the local characters. It's made a lovely break from the grind of University lecturing."

The evening finished off with Ruby playing her violin under the stars, previewing some of the ballads on Jed's new album. The sound swept and carried on the slight wind. It was thought Evan, a wonderful evening to round off what had been a wonderful visit for Ruby from Dr. Forster.

The mist which had started on Sunday, seemed to symbolically blow in on Dr. Forster's last day. Ruby was visibly tearful, when she had to make her goodbyes Wednesday lunch time.

"I'll be back," said Dr. Forster. "You see if anything can stop me visiting you and this place again. Now Ruby, you've got to work hard and concentrate on those finals girl, not long now!"

"Yes," said Ruby meekly, wiping her eyes. Evan put her arm protectively around her, and gave her a kiss. At lunchtime he took Dr. Forster up to Spring Farm in the

Land Rover. He had agreed the couple of hours off with Bill Clackett to take her back to the Priory valley. The mist was swirling slightly again, and Evan was pleased he could see her down the track safely.

They chatted on the way down:

"Your mother is a very lovely lady, Evan," she said.

"Yes, I am so lucky to have her, as my mum, I hope I appreciate her enough, she has done such a lot for Ruby as well. I wasn't the easiest child either with my obsession with The Hill!"

Said Evan.

"Yes, Ruby told me, but you've turned out OK. Some instinct told you that Hill was special, much as I imagine it stood out to the Saxon people who made it, too."

"I hadn't thought of that," mused Evan.

"Ruby tells me, that you didn't have much in common with your Dad, either, and that you look very different to him too?" She enquired.

"Yes, "replied Evan, "he was a good man, hard-working, but he had little time for me, exhausted from work no doubt, and we had little in common, and yes, we looked quite different too. He was stocky and dark, with dark brown eyes."

Dr. Forster looked at him quizzically. "Yet you look like a Viking, Vikings did raid the coast in Wales, and possibly came up the rivers too. Your mother is small and light, with mid brown eyes."

"Yes," replied Evan. "I guess I don't look like either of them really, but I hope I have or will develop some of my mum's good qualities anyhow."

"I think you already have," murmured Dr. Forster. "But it was more the genetics I was thinking about. You do know, don't you that with two brown eyed parents, you are genetically not going to have blue eyed. Meaning your father, was not your biological father, although he was your father in every other way."

It took a few moments to sink it, it made a lot of sense deep inside, he and his father had never really had a connection, and he really didn't look like his father, nothing about him and his father was physically similar. He had his mother's smile, and her aptitude to help others, her love of the countryside, and possibly a hint of her nose.... He paused.

"It makes a lot of sense," he said slowly. "We were very different in lots of ways. I'm an only child too, I know my mother wanted a lot of children but never could have them. She was grateful to have me...but I don't want to confront her, if she hasn't said anything all this time, I want her to carry her respectability to the grave with her. Best to let sleeping dogs lie as they say."

Dr. Forster nodded. "Wise words," she said.

They walked on half a mile in silence, Evan pondering about what he had just learnt. He didn't feel upset by it, or angry or resentful. He felt in some way relieved, as if things in his life were at last were beginning to make sense. Hid dad was dead and buried a long time back, let things lie. Only in his heart would he know a new clarity.

"There's just one thing," he turned to Dr. Forster. He had no idea why he was telling her this, perhaps he just wanted a sounding board? Or her approval? They stood there quietly on the track overlooking the magnificent ruined priory.

He took a large breath. "I'm going to ask Ruby to marry me, at the weekend in fact. I've booked

The holiday cottage at Spring Farm, where I left the Land Rover....I know I won't have a job in the Autumn, but I'll try really hard to find one and provide well for her…." Evan gulped. "I hope she will say yes!"

Dr. Forster took his hands. "Dear boy, is that is what's up? I knew there was something on your mind, I thought it must be The Hill of yours. You know I'm used to sorting out students' problems, and know when they have something on their minds. Do you think that Ruby is the type of girl who likes money? And is only bothered about you when you have it? She wouldn't have gone into archaeology, I can assure you if she only cared for money, it's paid a pittance, and the working conditions are tough, often extreme, cold, wet, unrewarding. No, with that brain of her she could have done something far more lucrative, been a lawyer or a surgeon. No, Ruby's not concerned about money. She's practical, you'll need somewhere else to live before winter comes again. But believe me, Evan, she likes you just as you are. Whatever happens you'll still have those strong shoulders, and resolve to do the right thing, won't you? You'll still want to love, support and care for Ruby. You'll still try your hardest to make everything work, even when times are tough, that won't change."

Dr. Forster squeezed Evan's hands and said. "She's one hell of a lucky girl. I'm sure she'll have you…..and if she doesn't you can ask me!" She laughed.

Evan laughed too, a huge weight seemed to lift from his shoulders, the black clouds of doubt parted. "Keep in touch, Dr. Forster." He said, "and thank you for everything, your visit has made the both of us so happy."

They shook hands and he watched for a while as Dr. Forster made her way down the track, the priory appearing and disappearing out of the gathering mist.

Chapter 10

That evening when Evan arrived back at the Shepherd's Hut, he told Ruby that he had booked Spring Cottage for that weekend. It was a bank holiday, so Ruby would be able to leave work Saturday afternoon at 4pm and then they could climb up to cottage, and spend Sunday and Monday there. Ruby immediately brightened up considerably at the idea, she had obviously been shedding the odd tear at Dr. Forster leaving, but trying to be brave. She gave Evan a big kiss.

"Thanks," she said, "thanks so much."

"Well we've not had a holiday and it's now late May, I thought a few days off would do us both good. I've got a real bargain of a deal too, because it wasn't let, it's just a bit too far off the beaten track for most people. Not near a shop or anything." Said Evan.

"Good," said Ruby.

Good thought Evan, the rouse of just a holiday had worked well.

"There's just one thing, we'll be climbing up there and back, it'll be more of an adventure that way."

"Great," said Ruby.

"It's only an hour's hike," added Evan, "And I don't mind carrying most of your stuff, you're just so fat, and your stuff is large and weighty!" he grinned. Ruby threw a cushion at him.

"Speak for yourself!" She joked.

Evan couldn't wait for Saturday evening to come, although he was very nervous too. IHe checked he had the Saxon ruby ring, three times, he didn't want to mess that up. He had already dropped off a bottle of Ruby's favourite red wine and groceries, when he had taken the Land Rover up to Spring Farm while returning Dr. Forster. His tummy had not flitted with butterflies so much, since he had first asked Ruby out on that dinner date at the Dragon and Dagger.

It was a fine evening, and Ruby stopped several times to admire the views over Brynafon and the valley.

"I should have come up here before," she said. "You can see everything! It's beautiful, and great to get an overall view of Brynafon. Ruby took out her camera to take a photo for Dr. Forster. "Look you can see Manor Farm, and the terrace houses and the school, you can even see the white blobs of sheep, and you can partially see the roof of the shepherd's hut, obscured a bit by that rocky out crop."

They climbed up the same prehistoric track that Dr. Forster had climbed down to find them on the Sunday. It was true it came on a slight diagonal down from Spring Farm to Brynafon. Occasionally used by walkers now, sometimes by trekkers on horseback and the odd mountain biker. If the weather was bad it was a hard track to see, and could be treacherous. Ruby admired the couple of upright marker stones Dr. Forster had told her about on their way up.

Evan had insisted he would do the cooking, cooking two fine steaks with asparagus and greens, and fresh potatoes. They had the meal on the terrace before the light started to fade. Evan had asked his mother to make them an apple crumble, which he had carefully carried up with him.

The sun was going down and was setting behind them. It was beginning to get cold; Ruby pulled her fleece down around her and shivered. Time to ask THE QUESTION, thought Evan.

He cleared his throat, his hands were clammy, he wiped them on his trousers. He swiftly took the ring in the little box he had for it out of his pocket, and producing it he looked Ruby straight in the eye.

It was now or never.

He took her small hands in his large ones:

"Ruby, will you marry me?" He asked. He'd gone over it a hundred times in his head. Keep it simple, he thought, it's yes.....or no. He hoped Dr. Forster had been right in her assessment of Ruby's character....

Ruby's eyes opened wide, she seemed to have gone even paler....then suddenly the colour rushed to her cheeks, and her face lit up with that flashing white smile.

"Yes," she said simply. "Yes, Evan, I will!" She leant forward and kissed him over the table.

Evan slipped the ring on her finger, it fitted as if it had been made for her. Ruby looked at it incredulously, she turned it over and over admiring the fine swirling pattern, polished red round stone and intricate mount.

"It's Saxon....Evan you must have found it at The Hill! It's amazing, stunning!"

"I did, I had it for a while, I have known I wanted to marry you for a while too, and when I found this ring under the nose of The Hill, I knew it would be just perfect for you. I know I should have given it in, Owain was fine about it, but this one thing I wanted to keep for you, for us." He replied.

"Let's go inside to bed!" She laughed. "It's getting cold out here – the dishes can wait!"

The rest of the weekend was a bit of a blur as far as Evan was concerned. They made love, they ate, they walked and they talked.

Ruby wanted to get married after her exams in the summer, which gave them just over a month.

She was adamant it had to be in the chapel with the Pastor, and Evan was delighted with that too.

"I think we just throw the wedding open and invite whoever wants to come in the village to the ceremony." Said Ruby.

Evan nodded. He wasn't into complicated weddings and they had little money between them, with what they had it was more important to put into better accommodation for them for the Autumn. They both agreed that.

"What about someone to give you away Ruby?" Evan frowned; her dad was obviously not a choice.

Ruby thought for a minute.

"Owain, it's got to be Owain, do you think he'll do it?" She asked anxiously.

"I am sure he will," replied Evan kissing her. "Mind you, it'll be the first time he's been to chapel since he was baptised! I'm not sure he has a suit or anything decent to wear at all." Laughed Evan. "The Pastor will be ecstatic!"

"Of course, your Mum's a definite, and Mary the Pastor's wife from the shop, the Clacketts and Jed and Nick, and your friends, who will be your best man?"

"Pete" said Evan. "He was always my best friend from school."

"Bridesmaids?" Asked Evan.

"Well, I've made friends with a lot of the young mums, and been asked to a few baptisms, so I'll see if I can rustle up a few tots. They've all got their nice party and special occasions dresses, so they won't need expensive brides-maid dresses. I am sure I can get Jo, one of the young mums to do some simple flowers, she's been selling some at the bakery in return for providing the table decorations, and we'll ask Jed to do the photographs."

"Good idea," agreed Evan.

It seemed deceptive simple. He had heard weddings were an expensive nightmare, and Ruby was not going to ask her father to fund the wedding. They would have to rely on what money had between them, which wasn't much.

"What about your Mum and brother?" Asked Evan, "that would put you in danger."

"No!" Said Ruby emphatically. "Not them, but there are a few special people from my old life I would like to invite, Dr. Forster, of course, if she is free, and the three nuns from my old boarding school. I guess I would have to write to them and explain the situation, they'll understand. I don't know if they'll come, but I'd like to invite them anyway."

It was agreed. The reception with a few invited guests would be at the bakery café, and anyone who wanted to could come and contribute with food or drink, or in any way they thought fit.

Evan would get all the formalities done, leaving Ruby time to study for her approaching exam and get her wedding dress.

The weekend went all too quickly as they descended hand in hand down the track to the shepherd's hut. Evan felt lighter and happier than he ever had in his life. He still didn't have a job from September, but he did have Ruby. For him his future had suddenly become a lot brighter.

Chapter 11

It was to be a week of changes in Ruby's and Evan's lives. Bill Clackett hadn't wasted time and the Brynafon Estate Agency was up for sale. Bill hoped to shift it by September.

It suddenly felt harsh and cold coming into work that Tuesday for Evan. The Estate Agency had been work and second home for Evan for the past nine years. He knew Bill wouldn't find a buyer at once, but it was and unpleasant feeling never the less. However, there was more interest shown than he had anticipated. At the end of the week a group of four locals came to see him. They had formed a co-operative to secure the shop. The local general shop was small and not particularly well stocked, and it was hoped that the addition of a chemist, post office if they could get a licence, and a grocer come general store, would be of benefit to the local community. It was hoped eventually to buy out the general store next door and make it all one. Evan happily registered their interest, and told them how long they would have to come up with the funds. The Brynafon Buy Outs as they called themselves, nodded and agreed terms. Serious fund raising was called for, and Evan found himself pledging £500 to the cause.

Mid-week Ruby came home from news from the bakery. Mary, the Pastor's wife, Evan's mother, and various of the other ladies in the village had made sure that Gwyneth, the bakery owner, had had a visitor every day during her stay in hospital. The operation on her broken hip had been successful, and Gwyneth had agreed with her daughter in Cardiff that she was now unfortunately too frail to live on her own. The good news was that Gwyneth's daughter had found a residential home for her near her, and nearer to her other daughter in Swansea too. A van would be arriving to take Gwyneth's personal effects to the home at the end of the week. Mary and Evan's mother would sort them out, and even more importantly the bakery would be sold too.

"We've got to buy it!" Said Ruby. "I can develop the bakery and café further, I know I can, I'm sure I can make more of a profit than we are now making, and Rhys's bread is selling well. There was even a mention of it in a Welcome Wales countryside magazine, apparently one of the journalists was walking round here, had tea at the café and a scone, and bought a loaf, and thought both were brilliant!

Evan, I know it's a lot but we just have to buy it. We'll need accommodation for the Autumn, and there are two rooms upstairs, we can use one as a sitting room and the other as a bedroom. The kitchen we can develop as part of the bakery, and there is a toilet and bath out the back – luxury!"

Ruby was right of course. Evan knew it, but it was a big investment and they would have to take a large mortgage, something he hated the thought of doing. But he had asked Ruby to be his wife, and this was the consequence of that action. He had to support her. So, with a large sigh, he agreed a price with Gwyneth's daughter and went to see his bank manager. He had enough for a deposit, but that left them well and truly out of funds. He didn't let the bank manager know his job was going, and Bill said nothing either. He would just have to find another job and quickly.

"No more meals out," he said to Ruby that evening. "We have to be even more careful from now on," she nodded solemnly. "I'll do a bit of sheep shearing for the next few weeks on a Sunday to help things along, you'll be studying anyway." He continued.

She nodded again. "Jed's album creation is coming up next weekend. He said he'd pay me a session rate, whatever that is, not a lot I suppose but something. I've got Sian coming in to cover me at the bakery for the day, I can get everything set up before I start anyway, we've not starting until 9a.m. which I'm told by Nick is very early for Jed, and we might have to drag him out of bed!"

Evan laughed. But on the whole, it wasn't a laughing matter, life had suddenly become a whole lot more complicated, expensive and daunting. Evan had always just lived one day at a time, cruising along in the slow lane happily. This was something he was unaccustomed to and unprepared for.

Evan couldn't sleep that night, he stayed awake worrying, mainly about his job prospects or lack of them. Having bought the bakery, it wasn't going to be possible to buy Bill Clackett's Estate Agency in the New Town, which was far more expensive. He wasn't really sure he wanted to anyway. He had really just drifted into Estate

Agency, and found himself rather good at it. But he'd never had a passion for it, or the business acumen and insight that Bill Clackett had. He'd never be half as good as Bill Clackett at it. No, he was better to get another job elsewhere, if only he could find one, the only two jobs he had seen so far, was Rhys's old job at the New Town industrial bakery, which Rhys had hated, or a job washing up in a seedy pub in the New Town, neither which appealed. He sighed, and turned over, his arm wrapped round Ruby's soft body. She slept soundly, she seemed infinitely more mentally resilient and strong than he was. He guessed the tough life she had had with her family had given her inner strength reserves; he didn't have.

Priorities, he would need a car, or a motor bike again, but he preferred a car if he could get a reliable one at the right price, he would ask Dave to look out for one for him. He could possibly ask Bill if he could buy the company Land Rover, but that would be expensive.

He turned, tossing the blankets and quilt off him. He quickly pulled it back over Ruby again. He would take the shower out of the Brynafon Estate Agency he had installed, and put it in the bakery, bathroom, that would save a bit of money. He'd do all the building work and decorating he could himself, he was sure he could do it; he was pretty handy, and Ruby, Ruby had the brains to make a go of the bakery, it had already improved under her management beyond recognition.

No, it wasn't just his lack of job prospects or buying the bakery that was gnawing at him. It was this intuitive feeling, like one he'd had for his Hill and Ruby. He knew in his heart what he really wanted to do; he'd know it for quite a while now. It had been brewing up within him for a time now, and all those trips to hill farms, to check on rentals and auction off farms had cemented the feeling. He knew exactly what he *wanted* to do. He wanted to be a hill farmer like Owain.

He turned over again. He would see if Owain would let him use his land, as well as The Hill to build up his own small heard of sheep, perhaps not just Lleyn sheep but more colourful coated ones as well. It made sense really, start small, gradually build up a bit. Perhaps even eventually train a sheep dog. Ruby would like that. They would never earn much; they'd have to think of other ways to make a living too. But he was sure Ruby had the brains for that too. He would have a long talk with Owain tomorrow after work. Owain was a good listener, he would run his ideas about a hill farm past him.

However, first, he needed to get another job to build this dream up. He needed most importantly to keep a roof over their heads, money for food and bills. It all seemed a lot of responsibility and a lot of worry. But he had the most important thing, he reminded himself. He had Ruby, Ruby and his Hill.

The next evening, he went to see Owain. Evan slipped into the kitchen through the back door as he did every night. Owain was asleep in front of the fire, which was unlit today. Meg, his collie, was sleeping at his feet. Evan shook his shoulder's gently to wake him up. Owain slept more and more nowadays. He was up at 5a.m. in the summer and asleep by 7p.m. sometimes he had a doze in the afternoon too. He was getting thinner too, he had become quite scraggy, the stout strong hill farmer had long since gone. Evan hoped Owain had had his tea that night. He worried about him, one day he thought, he would come in and would not be able to rouse him from his chair. He felt a tear prick his eye, but no, Owain would like that, he wanted to spend his last days here on his farm at Brynafon, not in a hospital or nursing home like Gwyneth.

The room smelt musty, Evan opened a window, going back he shook Owain's shoulder's again. He could see that Owain's pipe still smouldered on the small table beside him, he had not been asleep long.

"Owain, wake up, I need to talk to you!"

Owain stirred, and stretched, Meg stretched in unison with her master.

"Oh, aye boy, how long have you been standing there? Sit yourself down there and pass me a whisky lad."

"Owain, you have eaten haven't you and fed Meg?"

"Oh, aye, had a bit of cheese, ham and bread left over, Meg had half of it with me, we washed it down with a pint of beer, never you worry about me, boy."

But Evan did, although it must be said Meg looked perfectly happy on her rather unorthodox meal.

"So, what do you want to talk about boy?" Asked Owain puffing on his pipe again.

Evan took a big breath: "I want to be a hill farmer like you, Owain, I don't really want another ordinary job. I've got The Hill, and I want to start small and buy some sheep off you."

Owain puffed as his pipe some more, it blew across Evan's face in the draught from the window and Evan coughed.

"Close that window boy, you'll be letting all the warmth out!"

Evan did as he was told. Sometimes Owain took a time to come around to what he really wanted to say.

"About time, boy," said Owain. "I was wondering when you were going to come around to your senses, big strong lad like you, a waste in an office I say, and you've learnt from the best now haven't you!" It was a statement not a question. "Well, that will make life easier for me," continued Owain, "wondered what the heck I could give you and that lass of yours for your wedding present, not having many readies, but twelve good lambs I can do you. It's been a good year this year, we've not lost any lambs. I don't see why you and I can't run them all together, I've got no son or daughter to hand this land down to, so you might as well have the reign of it. Tomorrow we'll pick out some good lambs for you, and I'll look out a ram for you as well from my neighbours."

"Thanks' a million, Owain." Said Evan warmly.

"Mind you, you'll be needing a sheepdog too," warned Evan.

"I think I know where to get one of those from." Said Evan. Suddenly he was feeling better about life again.

Chapter 12

Evan ran Ruby up to Jed's at Manor Farm at 9a.m. on Saturday. She looked a bit nervous, but was very excited too. She kissed Evan goodbye and ran in like a school girl late for class, homemade violin case in hand.

She was relieved to find Jed was up, apparently Nick had dragged him out of bed, and he was having a coffee in the music room. Nick had set up the equipment the day before. Jed swiftly introduced her to the other violinist Benedict from the original Roaring Rainbows. Benedict was tall and elegant, with chinos, a white shirt, turned up at the elbows and cravat. Clearly the ravages of time had been kinder to him than Jed. He had not indulged in drink and drugs to the same extent. He put out a hand to greet Ruby. "Benedict Montague, at your service, young lady."

He was clearly quite a charmer too. The others were session musicians, who introduced themselves, a bass player called Tom, another guitarist called Rapper, and a drummer named Benson. To her surprise she found Tom would be playing not only an electric bass, but a double bass too, and Rapper would also sing. The only other female was Deryn, a Welsh harpist, who was playing on a few of the instrumental tracks, mainly with herself and Benedict.

It was all slightly daunting, although everyone was friendly enough and very professional thought Ruby, as they poured over their music, tuned up their instruments and had a run through of the songs in the morning. Ruby found she was fortunately not playing on the first two tracks, which was a relief as she could watch and learn from the others. Benedict expertly took her through the tracks he and her would be doing together. He was kind, patient, and business like, and she began to relax and enjoy herself under his tutorage. She was also surprised to find it was much easier to play alongside Benedict and the professionals, than it was her old school orchestra, or the University orchestra. With everyone else being a professional, they all knew what they were doing, everyone could sight read excellently, and they carried her along with them without a problem. She felt her playing improve throughout the morning, as she learnt techniques and phrasing from them. They also made sure they tuned up every couple of tracks, so everyone sounded in harmony, something rather missing from some of the orchestras she had played in!

They had a run through of the songs. Jed was clearly on fire, he was in command, he knew exactly what he wanted, sometimes he would stop and suggest a refinement, sometimes he would change the instrumentation about if he thought it suited the mood of the piece better. He nodded and winked at Ruby; she knew then she was doing OK.

Nick provided hot drinks and biscuits mid-morning, and Ruby was told to change into her red dress and do her makeup.

"Bring that violin case with you, as well as the violin, I can use them both." Said Jed as they went out to the wall of the barn. The light was falling gently on it. Jed asked Ruby to prop the violin case against the wall, Evan's homemade violin case which Ruby had painted in blue, with red roses, wild garlic and sheep on it, was going to star on the cover too. Evan would be pleased, she told Jed. Jed was as skilled photographer as he was a musician. She put her violin up to her shoulder to play, he asked her to turn slightly and shake her hair gently. Snap, snap, snap, Jed shot a couple of dozen photos of her.

"That'll do fine," he said and showed Ruby the photos. Ruby's sultry image stared back at her, violin in hand, hair tossed on the breeze, red dress and long pale legs.

"OK?" He asked Ruby. It was good of him to ask she thought.

"Fine," she said. Ruby could suddenly see why Jed had been so successful, he was super and multi-talented, but he was also passionate and focused about what he had to do. He had an eye for the detail, care for the musicians, making sure they all felt good about what they were doing, and understood what and why they were doing it. He made sure they all worked in harmony. He was the consummate professional, unlike the Jed who wandered round Manor Farm, got lost and forgot the time, when Jed worked, he was on it a hundred percent.

That afternoon they lay the tracks down, they would come back tomorrow if they needed too. The others were all staying overnight at Manor Farm to save time.

It was fast paced and exhausting, but the sheer adrenalin kept Ruby going, she thought she had never done anything so exciting, so exhilarating in all her life. At seven o'clock they had finished, she joined the others for a drink in the drawing room. Molly the cat sat on her lap and purred now the noise had finished. Ruby stroked her gently, she hoped she too could get a cat when they moved into the bakery.

"I like the music not to be too polished," explained Jed to her, "that way you keep the freshness and the excitement alive. I've decided on a name for the new band too," Rainbow Revival", and the new album will be called: "Pot of Gold." "

Ruby liked the sound of both. However even better was to come.

"I was really impressed with you today, Ruby," said Jed, "seeing it's your first time recording professionally…. I'd like to make you a permanent part of the new band along with Benedict of course. You'll be paid the Band rate today; I know that'll help a bit seeing you're getting married soon. I've taken the liberty as putting your name down as Red Davies on the credits. I hope that's OK, seeing you'll be Mrs Davies soon anyway, and Red will keep your anonymity. I've afraid I've already given one music magazine the impression you are a local Welsh girl, that should help diffuse any link with your family!"

Ruby gave Jed a big kiss, he had wonderfully thought of everything.

"We are also going to be touring in the summer, just a few days in Cardiff, Liverpool and Bristol to help promote the new album, and as the face of the Rainbow Revivals I'm counting you in, Ruby!" Jed continued.

Ruby nodded gratefully. She had learnt a lot today; she would sleep well tonight. She was nodding off already.

Jed nodded to Nick,

"Your chauffeur awaits you Rockstar chic!" smiled Jed.

Chapter 13

It was Ruby's archaeology final exams. There was a morning and afternoon session in Chester. Evan had driven her up the night before, and they had stayed overnight at a travel inn. Ruby had been fairly quiet on the journey, but had taken an interest in the surrounding countryside. They had wound their way up through the Welsh borders crossing over in Shropshire to England. Ruby seemed very calm though, the mere thought of academic exams terrified Evan. He had only just scraped passed most of his, but he knew Ruby was different. She wore his hoody up over her head as soon as they entered a built-up area. It stayed up when they checked in as Mr and Mrs Davies. Both Ruby and Evan knew that there was a chance that Ruby would be tracked electronically by her father when she took the exam. However, Dr. Forster hoped sitting them in Chester would throw him off the scent, and Dr. Forster had re-entered her as Ruby Davies.

Evan parked outside the University, and walked her in. They walked in silence hand in hand. Ruby seemed to be preparing herself mentally for the exams, he thought. He would meet up with her at lunchtime, she had an hour's break then before the afternoon session. He was going to get some provisions for them in Chester, and look around the city. He was keen to walk the city walls.

He left Ruby with a kiss, he thought he was more nervous for her than she was.

"It'll be alright, Evan" she said with a smile, then she turned and was off, through the double doors where he could not follow.

Suddenly he felt bereft without her. There was no warm delicate hand in his. He bit his lip, they had been together, side by side for nearly six months now, and suddenly she was gone, back into her world.

He looked around slowly, there was no sign of a motorcyclist on a classic bike, and no-one that looked like Ruby's dad in sight. The morning went fast enough for Evan, he bought provisions for them, and a few things they would need for their new home at the bakery, plus a present for Ruby. Chester was a very pleasant city indeed, and Evan was looking forward to walking the walls in the afternoon.

He was ready and waiting for Ruby at lunch break, and they had a meal in the student refectory which was cheap and cheerful.

"How did it go?" He asked somewhat anxiously.

"Fine," said Ruby over a bite of her ploughman's, and that was it.

Evan knew better than to press it, this was Ruby's way of handling the pressure, and she knew what to do. They sat outside, holding hands in the weak sunshine for the rest of the lunch break, and soon Ruby was gone again.

Again, Evan scanned the horizon, but thankfully no motorbike. The afternoon seemed longer although Evan enjoyed walking the walls, and visiting the local museum where Ruby had asked him to visit the Roman and Saxon sections, he was intrigued to find metal artefacts and coins like he had found on The Hill, he was even able to identify one of them. He noted there had been a large horde of coins found in Staffordshire.

He came out again, blinking in the weak sunshine. He decided he would go straight to the University and wait for Ruby there, he could have a coffee at the refectory while he waited.

It seemed a long wait even though it was just three quarters of an hour, and he was immensely relieved when he saw Ruby, hood up in his oversize hoodie, bounce down the steps to him. He gathered her up in his arms and swung her round.

"How was it?" He asked again.

"Easy!" she said.

"Easy?" He enquired dumbfounded.

"Easy!" she laughed.

Ruby had a spring in her step, as she left the University hand in hand with Evan. Neither of them noticed a black motorbike, with back leathered figure, in a black helmet, slowly cruise by behind them as they walked towards the parking. Nor did they notice the shot from a silenced gun, that whizzed past Ruby's ear as she manoeuvred to get into the passenger door, before burying itself unseen and unheard in the tarmac of the car park.

Chapter 14

The next weeks until the wedding past quickly. Evan's job hunt was still falling flat, but he consoled himself that soon Ruby would be his wife. Ruby had a new spring in her step and energy now that her exams were over. She positively bounced round like one of the new born lambs, Evan thought. She was pouring her energy into the bakery and café. She had an agreement with Gwyneth and Gwyneth's daughter that anything she made over the base line profit for the bakery and café was hers, and she was determined to do the best she could with it. Evan and herself were also allowed to make any alterations they wanted. It was all highly irregular but it worked for them.

Evan had been busy putting up notices for her in the village and put the word around, the bakery would be closed from 2p.m. on Saturday and work would begin on revamping it. If people wanted their daily bread to continue, would they please come and help on the renovations Saturday and Sunday? Ruby was unsure if it would work, but Evan knowing the generous hearts of his village was more hopeful, besides no-one would want to find themselves without bread on Monday morning for toast or sandwiches for work.

Firstly, the old serving counter was going to be ripped out, such a big serving area taking up a great deal of room was not needed. The café could then extend back, so that people had somewhere to sit indoors in cold weather and keep out of the rain. A good second hand rug went down in one corner, and Evan put up bookshelves, where a book swap library would give customers something to read, and somewhere to read it, while enjoying a drink and hopefully a scone, cake or light lunch. Money had been spent on a reconditioned wood burning stove that would also go on the west side of the café and keep the space warm and cosy. These was all Ruby's ideas.

They waited nervously to see if anyone would respond to their pleas for help. Pete and his new girl-friend Clara were the first to arrive, followed by Dave and Sian when Dave finished work. Rhys was also there wielding a sledge hammer efficiently, and Dave had borrowed a pick up for putting the debris in. After tea, a couple of young Mum's turned up, along with Jed, Nick and Owain. The room was soon knocked back. There was plenty of singing as debris was thrown into the back of the pick-up and at one point someone jokingly offered to throw Jed in as well!

The next morning most of the crew were back, with the addition of Evan's mum and the Pastor's wife Mary. Evan and Ruby had had to dissuade them quite vigorously from the heavy work. Evan was amused to see that the Pastor's wife had insisted to the Pastor that daily bread was very important, and she would be volunteering her services on a Sunday whether he liked it or not! Although the Pastor himself was seen sneaking in on Sunday afternoon to help!

The walls were re-painted, the floor mopped, and the remade and repainted units were put round the periphery. The kitchen/come bakery was given a makeover at the same time. Evan had managed to obtain a large pink American fridge, from someone who had not wanted to move house with it in the New Town, and it now had pride of place in the kitchen, allowing more storage for milk, cheese, cream and butter.

Evan's mum and Mary were running up some fresh curtains for under the counters and in the kitchen, with Evan's present to Ruby he had sourced in Chester, a large bale of colourful chicken printed material. A scrubbed-up table rescued from the tip in the New Town would be used to display wares that people wanted to sell, jams, cheese, flowers, and homemade soft toys and crafts. By six o'clock they had finished. Nick had bought a barbeque and they sat out in the front of the café with its newly painted white picket fence, with a Roaring Rainbows tracks blasting out, sizzling sausages and beef burgers grilling on the barbeque, and beer and wine flowing. It had been very tiring, but definitely well worth it.

Evan made a short speech to thank everyone, and there was a big clap as he said right now there was nowhere, he would rather be, or with people he would rather be with. It felt like the village had given Ruby and him the most terrific wedding present!

That week Ruby received an unexpected box in the post. Once more it was addressed to Evan at the Bill Clackett's Estate Agency and had been posted in Bath. Ruby opened the note that went with it first when Evan returned with it mid-week after work. The box was about 6 inches deep and 3 feet in length and took up half the bed in the shepherd's hut. The note said:

"Dear Precious,

This is for you; I hope it is acceptable. It's not new and it'll need alteration but I hope you can use it somehow, it's good quality and has never been worn. You'll find it hard to believe, I was slim and engaged once! My parents bought me this expensive wedding dress. However, I called the wedding off. It was the right choice, he turned out to be a drunken no-hoper, who has been thrown out of several university lectureships on account of his drinking! I've always seemed to be much better understanding the dead than I am the living! My elderly mother, in her nineties, would be delighted if you could use and wear it.

Of course, I'll be delighted to come to your wedding.

All my love

C.M.Forrester"

Ruby held it up against her, and swished it around as much as she could in the cramped space.

"It'll need a fair bit of alteration, but it's beautiful satin and pearls, do you think your mother could manage it?" Asked Ruby.

"I am sure between her and Mary, they'll do it." Said Evan. "Never having had a daughter, she's delighted to be getting a daughter-in-law.....Isn't it unlucky for the groom to see the bride in her wedding dress, before the wedding? " Asked Evan.

"But I'm not actually wearing it, silly," laughed Ruby, "and besides at the moment it's Dr. Forster's dress, when it is altered – then it'll be my dress!"

Evan laughed; Ruby could be so analytical at times!

Ruby stored it safely away in the box, once out is was difficult to put back, and satin and tulle puffed everywhere.

"I must remember to email Dr. Forster to thank her tomorrow." Said Ruby.

"I think we'd better go over to Mum's straight away with it," said Evan. "She won't have much time to work on it, dinner can wait!"

Things were changing fast for Evan and Ruby and it started with the acquiring of a family of sorts for them. One of the hill farms that Evan visited had had a litter of Welsh collies, they were cute brown and white and black and white bundles of fur. Evan had his eye on them for a few weeks, and made sure he saw them every time he was up at the farm. He knew the farmer from many years back, and he also knew that he had healthy, strong working dogs. He also knew that Nick was looking for a dog for Jed. So, having phoned Nick and checked his requirements, he agreed to purchase two.

For himself he chose a smart little female, black and white with a willing way about her. She was fairly small, which was good, because to start with she would have to share the shepherd's hut with them. He knew working dogs were meant to stay outside, but this was to be a pet for Ruby as well, she had expressed a strong interest in getting a cat and a dog when they were married. The pup would work with him, and cuddle with Ruby. For Nick and Jed, he chose a large brown and white male, with a laidback personality, who he thought would suit Jed and easily get used to Molly the cat, and be calm around her presence.

He knew a pup was not the usual wedding present, but Ruby was not your usual type of girl!

He picked them up at the end of the day, delivering the bigger pup to Nick and Jed. Nick had a tartan sturdy dog bed already installed under the kitchen table, a litter tray and a few good dog toys scattered around. Nick had had dogs while he was growing up, two greyhounds and a sheep dog and so was an experienced pair of hands. Jed had never had a dog before, but his calm manner, meant that they were inseparable from the first week.

"Aye, it'll probably have more common sense, than the old bugger too!" Said Nick as he cradled the pup in his arms in the kitchen.

"Be smarter too!" laughed Jed as he stroked the top of its furry head.

Evan had kept the kennel for their new pup hidden in Owain's barn, along with all the doggie paraphernalia. He was going to have to train this little one not to chase sheep pretty quickly, or hens come to think of it. It had a soft round bed made from an old grey and blue Welsh wool blanket, which he had hand sewed himself, and was stuffed with soft sheep's wool. He had taken the precaution of adding a canvas liner, so that the pup would not rip out the sheep's wool too easily. It was so comfortable, he thought he could easily sleep on it himself, and it would take Ruby curled up on it quite easily! It was going to be a squash in the shepherd's hut, but hopefully by September they would be in the bakery.

He had seen Owain training Meg and taken a keen interest, and he hoped with Owain's help to have his own little bitch well trained too.

There were initial squeals of delight from Ruby as he opened the shepherd's hut door, with the puppy in his arms.

"Sush," he said, "you have to be calm around dogs, especially puppies. You hold her a while," he said gently putting the pup in Ruby's arms, "while I get her bed, food and kennel up here."

"What are we going to call her?" asked Ruby. She was rubbing the puppy's coat with her face, tears of joys running down her face, the puppy licked her happily.

"That's for you to decide, it needs to be short, one syllabus so I can call her easily." Said Evan.

"Something Welsh," said Ruby. Ruby had a quick think. "Beth, I think."

Evan nodded approval.

"Be quick with the things, she's really wiggly!" laughed Ruby. The puppy seemed to be undertaking acrobatics in her arms, as it licked her face from various angles, and nibbled on her hair. "We'll take it up to Jed's regularly so the pups can play together."

"Good idea," agreed Nick.

It was early the next week Evan received a surprise phone call from Nick at his office.

"What's up Nick?" Enquired Evan, somewhat anxiously. Surely the puppy was OK, Nick wasn't calling to return it was he?

"Oh, little Bruce, that's what Jed's called the puppy after Bruce Springsteen, is fine, couldn't be happier, and everyone is bonding well. He's a grand little chap, very bright. I've had a few dogs in my time, but this one is by far the brightest, and a good eater, can fair pack it away. Yes, Jed adores him, no need to worry there, Evan, you did us proud. No, it's Molly the cat, I've called about."

"Don't they get along?" Asked Evan still worried.

"Oh, they are just managing fine, after the first hiss to assert her authority, Molly was fine with him, no it's not that, Molly has had kittens. So, do you want one? There's five good little kittens, three black and white and two black. I know Ruby was after a kitten, it'll be a couple of months yet till they are ready to leave their mother, of course, but it would be part of our wedding present for you both." Nick sounded like Molly having kittens was all in the run of things.

"Goodness, I didn't know Molly was pregnant!" Said Evan surprised.

"No," said Jed, "neither did we! We've never seen another cat round here at all, so goodness knows who the father is! But Jed's quite used to that rock and roll lifestyle! So, we'll keep a couple of kittens for mousing, there's bound to mice and rats now we've got Bronwyn's and Claire's horses here with all the feed."

There was a pause, then Nick continued. "Guess we'll have to get Molly neutered when the kittens have gone, thought she was neutered like, but we never knew where she came from when she turned up here, thin and hungry, and Jed fed her our salmon tea!"

"We'll come over and chose one then!" Said Evan. "I'll let Ruby chose the one she wants."

"Great," said Nick, "get Ruby to bring her violin so she can have a bit of a jam with Jed, oh and see if Owain wants to come as well, we'll make a night of it."

"Great!" Replied Evan. "Friday OK?"

"See you then." The phone went down. Life was full of surprises.

Chapter 15

The day of the wedding dawned fair. A mixed Spring was turning into a good summer that year. Evan's stag night had consisted of a couple of cokes at the Dragon and Dagger with Pete and Dave, Jed, Nick and Owain. It was all he wanted. But it was good night, with everyone in high spirits. The landlord had even given them a round on the house. It was also probably the first time the Dragon and Dagger had seen three nuns drinking at the bar. One nun was large and strong, and looked a bit like a man in drag Evan thought, if he hadn't known better. One was frail and elderly in a wheel chair, but still downing more than most at the bar, and the other was a small elderly lady, who was seriously rivalling her wheelchair bound companion with the Guinness! The two smaller ladies had pronounced Irish accents, and talked fast and furiously, the man like nun was quieter and drank little, but was taking in all her surroundings with interest, before getting into deep and knowledgeable conversation with a local farmer on the merits of a Massey Ferguson tractor over a John Deere.

Evan ducked out to introduce himself as the groom. There were warm and a very strong handshake all round from the amazon nun. Evan found himself thinking that his rugby team at school might have done better with that particular lady on its side.

"We couldn't miss it," said the elderly sister in the wheelchair, "not our Ruby getting married, God bless her, and you young man."

When he had a minute, he looked round for Dr. Forster, but he didn't see her anywhere. He frowned, perhaps she was camping out on the hills, most likely. He fervently hoped she'd be there tomorrow for Ruby's sake.

Ruby went to Jo's, one of the young mum's houses for her hen night, and after Jo had put the children to bed, they and a couple of other young mum's, and Sian, watched a chick flick with an Italian red wine, TV was a luxury for Ruby at the moment.

Mary, the Pastor's wife and Evan's mum had been invited but they were gallantly struggling to finish the dress. Jo, who had been a florist, was creating a lovely white fresh flower wreath for Ruby's hair, which would accentuate her shiny dark locks to maximum effect. The morning of the wedding the mums and children were gathering white flowers from the gardens and hedge rows, plus blossom to act as confetti. It was all in hand. Ruby was getting ready at the Pastor and his wife's house, which was handy. The shepherd's hut being far too cramped and muddy. Evan was getting ready with Pete at his mum's house. No costly transport was required. Evan had used some of the more bent up gold found on the Hill, as a wedding ring. The local jeweller had fashioned it into a ring, and Evan had a Celtic design he hoped Ruby would like etched into it. Evan had washed his one and only suit, which was fortunately a shiny dove grey, it was showing wear round the cuffs now, it was only the second suit he had ever owned, but he had neatened it up and bought a dove grey bow tie and new white shirt while he was in Chester. He wasn't sure he would need a suit in his next job, so he didn't want to splash out for a new one, beside he was sure everyone would be looking at Ruby, she would no doubt look stunning. He had polished his shoes until they shined though and made sure he looked as neat and groomed as he could. His mother had given him a big hug, she was proud of her boy.

He had a few nerves, but not many, once Evan made his mind up to do something that was that, and he was a lot less nervous than when he had first asked Ruby out, and when he had proposed.

He stood quietly in the chapel with Pete at his side. The sun was streaming in the window. The organist was playing "When sheep safely graze," by Bach on Ruby's request. The little chapel was squashed full, there was standing room only, it looked like most of the village had turned up. There was a buzz of eager anticipation.

He heard the doors of the chapel open, and light streamed down the aisle. For Evan it seemed symbolic that light had flooded into his life, in the form of Ruby. He turned as Ruby gracefully walked down the aisle on Owain's arm. Owain was beaming from cheek to cheek. Evan had never seen him so animated and happy. Owain wore a country/shooting type green tweed suit with a matching waistcoat, breeches and mustard coloured shooting socks, and smart brown brogues. The suit looked a trifle hot and a little tight, Evan grinned to himself and wondered where he had dug that up from, he didn't think Owain had processed a suit, or a pair of smart brown brogues. However, all eyes were on Ruby. She looked like a screen goddess. The satin dress came to her ankles, gracefully moving with her, the pearl bodice had short sleeves, looked simple, elegant and expensive, and Ruby carried it off superbly. On her hair was entwined wreath with hedge parsley, small white roses, and green stalks woven exquisitely round. It was a beautiful, fresh and showed off Ruby's dark shiny hair to its best. She carried a simple bunch of matching white roses, lily of the valley and hedge parsley tied with a white ribbon. Two little bridesmaids and a page boy came after her, accompanied by one of the mother's and on a white ribbon lead, Beth the sheepdog pup almost rolled along. Evan thought it was probably the first time the chapel had seen a dog at a wedding. He smiled; it was a nice touch.

The service seemed to fly by, and he was soon placing the wedding ring on Ruby's finger and kissing her. Then they were out into the bright sunlight and across the road to the café.

They found the café had been decorated with white balloons and ribbons, and here Jed insisted they all paused for the photographs. He went this side and that, zoomed in and out with the camera lens, and took the usual formal photographs, together with a lot of more fun informal ones.

Evan was amazed at the transformation of the café, there were simple white paper cloths covering the tables, that had been assembled in a long horse shoe shape. On the tables were clear bottles, each with frothy white hedge parsley in them, the whole place sparkled in the sun. There were bottles of champagne, a present from Jed and Nick, on which a toast to the bride and groom was proposed by Pete, who proceeded to give a short speech to the assemble village, even more people had seemed to have turned up. As the café was still open and Rhys was holding the fort, there was also assembled hikers and bicyclists, who were quite enthralled by the proceedings.

"We never thought our Evan, would do it!" Began Pete. "To find a girl who was as bonkers about The Hill as he is! Who approved when he bought it, instead of buying her a house! Who wouldn't mind living in a shepherd's hut with him – but he has, and what a girl!

Ruby came to our village in the most dismal of circumstances, but no she didn't let that get her down. She straight away found a boyfriend, got a job in the café, and proceeded to transform it to the meeting place you see now. Not only that, she helped our dear Pastor start a mother's and toddlers' group at the chapel, and the chapel hasn't been so full for years. She's a gifted violinist as well as an archaeologist, and has brought vibrancy to the music at chapel too. Also, I hear she's starring on Jed's new album and is the cover girl for the new re-formed Rainbow Revivals. She's not just been busy there, that Hill I talked about, well she invited an eminent Professor of Archaeology along to look at it," he motioned to Dr. Forster who had appeared and was sitting next to Ruby, "and guess what, he wasn't mad after all! The Hill really is something special, probably Saxon!"

There was a hearty round of applause.

"So, here's to our Evan and Ruby, may they have a long, happy and wonderful married life together! Evan and Ruby!"

Everyone raised a glass, and there was another noisy round of applause. It looked like the whole village had turned up to the wedding of the year!

"You look beautiful, Ruby," beamed Dr. Forster and she gave Ruby a big hug. "The dress really suits you; I've taken some photos for my elderly mother."

"Thank you so much," Ruby hugged her again. People were greeting and hugging her from all sides, she was quite overwhelmed. "Evan's mum and Mary, the Pastor's wife worked flat out to alter it for me. Where were you staying, Evan said he didn't see you at the pub?"

"Oh, with Jed, he kindly said I could stay anytime I wanted, so I took him at his word." Ruby turned, she wasn't sure, but she thought she could detect a warmth in the smile between Jed and Dr. Forster, wonders would never cease!

The three nuns, had joined her now and they talked excitedly kissing Ruby fondly.

"I'm so very glad you could come!" Exclaimed Ruby.

"So are we," said Mother Prioress, "We were determined to get here, and I must admit the accommodation and the food at the Dragon and Dagger, has been far better than we anticipated, and you child look beautiful, and what a fine young man you have."

Evan was surrounded by his mates, Owain and his mother, and the Clacketts. Ruby turned and grabbed his hand and kissed him again. Evan, his mother thought, had never looked happier. Indeed, he had never felt happier. Evan's mum also thought to herself, she had never had a happier or more proud time since he had been born.

Guests had each bought a platter to share, and the Mary and Sian uncovered the plates and set them on the tables. There was a feast, and if that wasn't enough Nick was turning a wild hog roast on a spit, and slicing bits off for everyone.

"I shot that wild boar myself, up above The Hill it was, a few days ago," Said Owain proudly, "and Nick said he could roast it, so that is part of our wedding present to you!"

Evan turned to Ruby, raising his glass to her:

"Here's to us!" He said.

"To us!" Said Ruby.

They spent the first night of their honeymoon in the shepherd's hut, and the next morning hiked up to the cottage at Spring Farm to spend five days together. Evan was longing to spend time alone with Ruby, life had seemed so frantic lately, and what with her studying for her exams and rehearsing and making the album with Jed, and him working on Sundays sheep shearing, and making her a surprise wedding present in Owain's barn, time for them to just be themselves together had been woefully sparse.

They made love, laughed, talked, walked and generally just enjoyed being the two of them. Other people were surplus to requirements. The weather had stayed fair, and Evan wanted to show Ruby the beautiful Benedictine ruined priory in the next valley, something she had not seen yet. It was set beside another river, and it had sweeping lawns around it, and terraces up the hillside. It was a romantic and historic, and he was sure Ruby would like it.

She did, "It's beautiful, stunning! Thank you for showing me Evan, I had no idea we had this on our doorstep!" They wandered hand in hand round the cloisters and the ruined nave of the church. Ruby took copious photos. She exclaimed patiently to Evan about the night stairs, and the day stairs the monks took at different times to get down to the priory. The terraces for growing vines, the fish pond to keep the monks stocked with fish, and where the gardens would have been that grew herbs for medicine and food.

"This would have been a guest house and a hospital too, and being Benedictine a centre for education and learning. It was inspired by the rule of St. Benedict, an Italian priest and monk from the 6th Century. The area would have supported farms and local people. The foundation often grew rich, but this was quite a small place, compared with the large abbeys in Yorkshire, Riveaulx for instance."

"It's great to have someone with me to explain about it," said Evan. "I'd only just walked around it before and thought it atmospheric."

Ruby squeezed his hand and smiled. Evan was pleased he'd had success at his first tourist outing with Ruby.

"You know, Henry V111th was one of the biggest vandals in history, him an Oliver Cromwell later, when he destroyed all these abbeys and monasteries to fund himself. I often wondered what happened to all the monks and nuns who lost their homes and occupations, what did they do? Where did they go? What happened to all the farms that supported the abbeys and priories?

Evan knew the feeling, but he kept it inside him, he didn't want to put a dampener on their visit.

They had an ice cream, and Evan took several photos of Ruby. He realised he had none of her at all, although Jed would provide some from the wedding. Ruby bought two slate table mats, and two coasters from the small gift shop, and admired the Welsh wool blankets that stacked the shelves. She looked round for some time, gaining ideas of extra things she could sell at the bakery.

They splashed out on a cream tea in the little tea room that overlooked the river and water meadows. Swallows dipped and dived for insects nearby.

"Oh, can we walk in the water meadows, they are just so beautiful, I've never seen so many flowers all together. They're just a piece of heaven. I can see why the monks chose to live here!"

"Sure," replied Evan, as they walked hand in hand along the flowery swathe. "We've come just at the right time of year you know, in a couple of weeks they will have finished and set seed."

Ruby took many more photographs.

The next day they hired a double canoe, and canoed downstream to the next village. Both Evan and Ruby had done limited canoeing, but after a few close encounters with over hanging willows on the banks they managed. Half way down they stopped at a small secluded water meadow, enclosed by forest on either side. Here they dragged the canoe up the bank.

"Want to make love in a meadow, Ruby?" Asked Evan hopefully.

"You bet!" Was the answer.

Later on, they had the picnic Evan had prepared earlier, Welsh goats' cheese with chives, ham and seeded bread, washed down by an elderflower cordial.

"Delicious!" Announced Ruby. "I'd quite an appetite after all that.....canoeing!" They both laughed.

They dropped the canoe off at the next little village, where it would be ferried back by transport. Then set off up a steep climb to a ridgeway track that followed high above the course of the river back up to the Priory, dropping down on an old stone mediaeval track to the Priory itself.

"It's busier and more habited here, than Brynafon," stated Ruby.

"Well, there was a real railway here once upon a time, and the land has more water meadows. It's not such a steep gorge as at Brynafon, there are more opportunities to farm beside the river. At Brynafon there are no low pastures, just the scarce hill tops. This was a better place to farm and prosper in." Stated Evan

Ruby nodded. She had learnt from Evan today.

They were pretty tired by the time they hiked back up to Spring Cottage.

"A lie-in, I think tomorrow." Said Evan.

"A long lie-in," agreed Ruby. In fact, the next day it rained, so they stayed in bed all day.

The rest of the honeymoon consisted of a trip up the river in a glass topped sightseeing boat, walking to see a deserted village, and a trip to the heritage water mill and centre, where Rhys procured the stone ground wheat for the bakery.

Ruby introduced herself and Evan to the heritage centre manager. The manager was delighted to make their acquaintance, the regular order for wheat was making a big difference to the centre, particularly keeping the water mill open. Learning, that it was their honeymoon, the manager provided them with a cream tea at the farmstead tea room, on the house.

They sat there under a parasol enjoying the sun and the surroundings, the heritage centre consisted of old farm buildings, with craftsmen and women working in their shops, and a general gift shop.

"I'd like to buy something for your Mum, Mary and Jo, they've been brilliant to us, especially your Mum helping with my dress and the wedding. You know Evan, you're very lucky to have a Mum like yours." Said Ruby.

"I know," smiled Evan, "I probably hadn't appreciated the fact until I met you, and now she's your Mum too."

Ruby smiled. It took her some time to source three small gifts, some lavender scented bags for Mary, a crocheted hat for Jo, and a pretty hand painted scarf for Evan's mother, in a lavender colour she knew she wore. The shop wrapped them up for her prettily.

"I could spend all day here, it's lovely." Said Ruby. "I'd love to develop our bakery and tea rooms more, perhaps one day. You know Evan, we've had the most marvellous honeymoon, and we've been so lucky with the weather too. I couldn't have been happier, than I have been here with you!" She gave him a big kiss.

Evan swung her round lifting her off his feet. Somehow, he knew with Ruby that life would be OK. As long as he had Ruby, they'd be fine. Jobs came and went, but Ruby, Ruby was for keeps.

They walked back hand and hand, crossing a pretty stone humped back bridge with ducks swimming under it, and continued walking back along the old railway track overhung with magnificent beech trees. For Evan, too it had been a wonderful honeymoon.

Chapter 16

The honeymoon ended all too quickly, and they back at the shepherd's hut. It was quiet, Nick had been looking after Beth with Jed's puppy, Bruce. Beth would be returned on the Sunday, apparently the sibling puppies had had a wonderful time continually playing together until they wore themselves out and fell asleep on the floor at the Manor, or wherever they found themselves!

There were other changes too. For Evan, the most notable one was that Dave had become engaged to his Evan's childhood friend Sian.

"It was about time I popped the question," said Dave, as he, Evan and Pete shared a drink at the Dragon and Dagger.

"She's a great girl, I'm really happy for you, Dave," said Evan. This round was most definitely on him.

"Yeah, well work is steady at the garage, I'm doing alright, and I'm going to try to buy one of the terraces in the village, when one of the families moves out to those new houses."

Evan was reminded, that the conversions of the last side barn at Manor Farm was nearing completion, and the two village families would be in there in the next couple of weeks. The houses in the village would be ready by the end of summer.

"I'll let you know when something turns up." Nodded Evan.

Pete though, was looking a bit dejected. He and Clara hadn't lasted long.

"She wasn't impressed with doing up the café," said Pete. "Said I was as much fun as a wet weekend and ruinous for her nails. She was high maintenance too." Pete looked dolefully into his beer. He'd never had much luck with women.

"I'm sorry, mate." Said Evan, Dave nodded agreement.

"I just don't know what I'm doing wrong. You two have got two great looking, lovely girls. I'd spent a fortune on Clara in the two weeks, we'd gone out, trips to the cinema, meals out and two new dresses off me!" Pete was looking even more forlorn.

Evan was genuinely sorry for Pete, he was a nice guy, too nice perhaps, and gullible. Evan looked a Dave.

"Do you want to tell him, Evan, or shall I?" Said Dave slipping the dejected Pete another beer.

Evan took his cue. Clara had been high maintenance and demanding, you could see it in her nails, heavy make-up, coiffured coloured hair, expensive up to the minute clothes and handbags.

"She could see you coming, that one." Said Evan. "Look mate, you've got it the wrong way around, you're the average guy, that thinks girls are all about looks, that they'll be as lovely on the inside, as they look on the outside. Believe me mate, once you've been cooped up in a shepherd's hut with a girl for six months, you'll soon find that temperament counts for more than beauty. I'm not saying get a cart horse of a girlfriend, but mate. You see long legs, tits, and a toothy smile, and your brains just take a nap."

Evan paused then went on. "Bill Clackett, my boss, learnt the hard way about that one. He married one like Clara, nearly bankrupted him, then she left him for another estate agent who was better off than him. But now he's really happily married to Margaret, she's a lovely woman all round. Trust us your better off without the likes of Clara!"

Dave nodded in agreement.

Evan continued: "Next time engage that brain of yours, and look at what they're really like, not just the packaging they come in!"

Pete looked crestfallen, took a few gulps of beer, but then rallied a little.

"Thanks," he said, downing the rest of the pint. "It's good to have mates like you two."

He wouldn't make the same mistake again he thought. Next time he was going to ask a whole lot more questions, and really talk to the next girl, find out what she was really like, before he got in over his head. Perhaps he'd even run the next one past Ruby, she didn't miss a thing. He was beginning to feel a lot happier already. He was definitely over Clara, and good riddance he thought.

Evan found Ruby smiling over the wedding photos when he arrived home that night. She was sprawled on the bed wrapped in her dressing ground, giggling over a large album Nick had dropped in to her that evening.

"Look," she said, "this one's a cracker!"

As well as the standard wedding photo line-up at the front of the album, there were more informal shots at the back. People pulling faces, off guard moments with little bridesmaids throwing jelly at each other. Owain, snoring loudly, lolling in a chair, Ruby and Evan having a kiss, but the one Ruby was laughing at, was of a small furry white and black bundle, Beth, on her hind legs licking the bottom of the wedding cake.

"I don't think anyone noticed!" Laughed Evan. He pulled Ruby towards him, and shut the album putting it on the side. "I think I could do with some marital action here!"

Ruby giggled and obliged.

It was Saturday and Ruby was back to work. She was surprised to find a whole stack of wedding presents waiting for her in the bakery.

"People just kept handing them in!" Exclaimed Mary.

"Goodness," said Ruby. "I really hadn't expected anything after all the help we got with the renovations of this place." The café and bakery were now much easier to work in with the counter smaller and set back. They were busy too, many people tempted out by the good weather. Day trippers from the New Town and surrounding towns, and the usual walkers and cyclists were in abundance. Claire and Bronwyn and ponies with hacking guests, were also making it a regular stop over point at the end of their ride out.

It was shortly after the lunch time rush, when a tall man approached Ruby with an order. She took it, asking him to take a seat at one of the tables. There was something vaguely familiar about him, she glanced in his direction again. He was tall with broad shoulders, with grey wavy hair, blue eyes and had an unremarkable English accent. He was dressed in beige chinos, and had a white open neck shirt on, with a red spotted cravat. He held a panama hat in one hand.

Odd, thought Ruby. But she had a good memory for faces, and she was sure she had never seen this guy before. He wasn't one of her father's military friends that he would occasionally bring to the house, and he wasn't from the University either.

She came over to his table with his coffee and a scone.

"Have you been here long?" he asked her. If this was a chat up line, this guy was making a big mistake. She made sure he saw her ring hand, as she let it linger as she put down his side plate with a scone on.

"A while," she said non-committally. Should she run now, had he been sent by her father?

"So, you'd know if there is a Meredith Thomas still living here?" He asked.

Ruby frowned. It hadn't been what she had been expecting. This chap wasn't interested in her at all.

"There is a Meredith here...." She paused. "But her surname isn't Thomas, I'll ask for you."

Ruby went back into the café. It was Mary she saw first.

"There's a chap over there," she gestured to the table. "Wanting to know if there is a Meredith Thomas here?"

"There is," said Mary. "But she's not called that now." She beckoned Evan's mum over.

"Meredith, that chap over there is asking for you by your maiden name."

Evan's mum turned, she all but dropped the tray of cups and saucers she was carrying.

"It can't be!" She said. She had gone quite red. "I think it might be!"

Without an explanation, she went over to the table, and quietly sat down opposite the gentleman.

"Clive?" She asked. "Clive, it is you!"

"Yes, Meredith, my dear, I'd recognise you anywhere, as lovely as ever. I still see the girl in your eyes." He paused "and married I presume." He said glancing at her wedding and engagement ring Evan's mum still wore.

"Widowed, many years now," she corrected. "But I have a lovely son, recently married to Ruby over there, called Evan."

Evan's mum, glanced back toward the curious Mary and Ruby.

"I've got to get back to work." She said hurriedly.

"But I can take you out to a meal this evening, can't I? We've a lot of catching up to do I imagine. I'm staying at the Dragon and Dagger."

Evan's mum nodded.

"Seven thirty," she said.

"I look forward to it," said the gentleman. He finished his coffee and scone and left.

"Old friend, from way back." Said Evan's mum, and she refused to say another word about her gentleman stranger.

"That's strange!" Said Evan, when he came back from work and Ruby told him. "No, don't know him at all, never met him. English, you say? I didn't think she knew many English people. But I know she worked for some months in The New Town when I was young, about five or six. My dad was injured in an accident at work and mum took a shop job there to pay the bills. It's probably someone from those days." Evan thought no more about it.

"Funny," said Ruby. "He looked ever so slightly familiar, but I just can't place him. But he's taking your Mum out for a meal at the Dragon and Dagger tonight."

"Good," said Evan. "Mum deserves to be treated, and goodness knows, I'm sure I haven't treated her enough!"

Evan had some news too: "You know we didn't get a wedding present from the Clackett's, I thought it a bit strange, but figured he'd just not got around to it, and he's been so generous to me I wasn't going to mention it." They had been unwrapping all the wedding presents, and Ruby had been meticulously writing a list of whom had given them what, so she could thank them. There was a large mound of presents stacked at the end of the Shepherd's hut, that Evan was going to take and store at the bakery tomorrow.

"But, he hadn't forgotten," continued Evan, "he just hadn't got around to completing the paper work.... guess what....the Land Rover is our wedding present!"

"Wow!" said Ruby. "That's just so generous of him!"

"That's Bill," said Evan. "I don't think I'll ever find another boss or friend like him in a million years!" Evan didn't know yet just how right he was.

That Sunday, Evan's Mum asked Ruby to give a message to Evan, could he come over at 12noon. Evan duly attended, thinking his mother must want help with something. But instead the tall stranger was there.

As Evan walked in, the stranger held out his hand to him, with a warm open smile. Evan stopped on the spot....same height, same broad shoulders, same wavy hair, albeit the stranger's hair was grey, same blue eyes and same smile. Evan took a deep breath; he knew in his heart who this was.

"Evan, I know this might be hard for you, and come as a shock, but this is Clive Jenkins....your biological father."

It all came out over lunch. Ruby had joined them by this time. It was before Evan's mum had been married, just. Evan's father had been considered a solid prospect by his mother's family. He was hard working, a teetotaller, and was a solid stoic sort of man, not given to violence or chasing women. But it must be acknowledged, he was boring. He scarcely spoke to Evan or Evan's mother, and his idea of fun after a hard day's manual labour was to read the newspaper. Occasionally, he went fishing. It was more a marriage of convenience than love. Evan's mum came from a poor family of six children, it was her duty as the eldest to relieve the family of the burden of herself as quickly as possible. She had a pleasant countenance and demeanour, was sensible, could cook, and was good at looking after a home and siblings. So, she had taken the first solid proposal of marriage she had been offered at sixteen.

Then, she had met Clive Jenkins. He was an English salesman, passing through Brynafon to sell domestic cleaning wares. Evan's mum had bought a few, and they had chatted and got on like a house on fire. But Evan's mum was getting married later that week, and Clive was off round the country selling his wares. For once in her life, for one wonderful afternoon, Meredith Thomas, had done something rash. Then he was gone, and Evan's mum had dutifully married her husband. She had cherished her memory of Clive all that time, keeping her guilty but glorious memory safely locked within.

"It was just as well," said Evan's mum, matter of factly. "It turned out I could never have a child with my Bryn. If I had not had the fling with Clive, I would never have been childless, but I had you, Evan. I don't regret that for one minute. It was so close to the wedding, at first, I wasn't sure who's baby it was, but as the years went on, I knew that Clive here, was your biological father, and my husband was sterile."

Clive grasped Evan's mum's hand. "I never forgot you, Meredith, not for a day. But I was selling my wares up and down the country. I didn't get back to Wales for two years. By that time, it was too late."

"I'd like this just to be let lye," said Evan's mum firmly. "Just kept between us. There's no need for anyone else to know, it's none of their business."

Ruby and Evan nodded. So, thought Evan. Dr. Forster had been right after all.

Clive Jenkins stayed in the village, first at the Dragon and Dagger, then renting Spring Cottage, then moving in with Evan's mum. Evan was pleased for her to have company. He found that he and Clive had things in common, they both liked walking, they both liked being out and about and their temperaments were similar. Evan was to find out, that he liked Clive. He enjoyed getting to know him, his company and spending time with him having a drink at the Dragon and Dagger. But most of all he was glad his mother, was very, very happy indeed, and he could not begrudge her that.

Chapter 17

There was another person staying in the village as well. University term had ended for Dr. Forster, and after a week's holiday in Greece, she headed back to Brynafon, this time bringing her small pale blue 4x4 Fiat panda car with her. Jed had wittily named it "the powder puff," and it was gingerly driven up the bumpy track to the Manor Farm where Dr. Forster was staying as Jed's guest. It was another, very unexpected relationship that seemed despite all the differences appeared to be flourishing.

Ruby had arranged that children from the local primary school at Brynafon, would be digging a trench at the bottom of The Hill field, where the field met the terraced cottages, with Dr. Forster supervising. The next week, two further group of youngsters would arrive from the secondary school in the New Town, to finish off the trench. The far north of the field boundary was being left, but digging would start from Owain's farm to the bottom middle test pit, where artefacts had been found. As there was a natural drainage slope down to, and past Owain's farm, it was felt that artefacts would have drained from The Hill to between those two points.

Dr. Forster had demonstrated a fall line to the children, by getting them to roll little stones down from under the nose of The Hill. One wit, said he fell down one of those frequently when he was skiing! Undaunted by the rainy weather, the children adorned in water proofs and bright coloured wellies dug enthusiastically. Ruby, who was working, offered the café for free hot chocolates and chocolate biscuits for everyone and put on the new wood burning stone so that the children could dry off. A line of small brightly coloured welly boots stood outside the café drying out. It was so wet, that by the afternoon it was decided that the children would wash the finds with old toothbrushes in plastic boxes set up under the parasols of the café tables. The children became even wetter as they splashed about.

"I thought child slave labour had been outlawed!" Commented Evan to Ruby, when he popped in for a cup of tea that afternoon.

"Most are loving it, and tell me it's much better than school, only two have gone back to lessons." Said Ruby. A fair amount of blue and white Victorian pottery was found, and some 1940s brown and green wares. The children particularly liked the sheep teeth they found, and their best find was a ram's horn, none likely to be particularly old. One boy found a rusted pen knife Owain had lost in a storm several years back, but the star attractions were the five Saxon gold coins. These were carefully washed and inspected. The children made rubbings of them and took photographs for a display on the class room walls. They were also allowed to keep the sheep's teeth and ram's horn.

"Real nuggets, pieces of eight, pirate treasure!" Announced one boy.

"Not pirates, but Saxons!" Said Dr. Forster.

"Did the Saxon's wear the ram's horn on their helmets?" Asked another little girl.

"No," corrected Dr. Forster gently. "Those pictures you see with horns are of Vikings are incorrect, although you are correct that the Saxons and Vikings were round at the same time, the Vikings never really wore horns on their helmets. They might have drunk from ram's horns though, as might the Saxons. Horns on helmets would have meant the helmets were too easy to knock off in battle. No, that is just a Hollywood films inaccuracy!"

Ruby was amazed at her enthusiasm and patience with all the children, she had a natural rapport with them. A different class from school was helping every day, fortunately the weather improved to just showers after the first day.

The next week, the last week of the school term, saw the two teams from the New Town secondary school arrive, and serious barrow loads of earth were removed, then back filled as they dug back towards the middle test pit.

Dr. Forster showed the teenagers how to dig in layers, and record their finds. The young curator, Christian Blake, from the museum came to see their progress, and talked with them about the Saxons in general. He was so keen that he came up three lunchtimes. The local press, The New Town News, also came and took photographs of the event. For most of the young people it was a welcome relief from exams and school work.

"I just like being out of the class room," said one young man. Finds dribbled out and were carefully recorded. As they went down deeper more gold coins came to light, seven in total, plus more gold pins, another squashed torque, a belt buckle, a ceremonial gold arrow head, and the best find another elaborately worked brooch, all Saxon. Further down still were several arrow head and thin projectiles, all prehistoric. Dr. Forster explained out the layering, and how the oldest things were usually furthest down, if the soil had not been disturbed, and how leather and wood did not survive. Also, how unusual it was to find Saxon remains, as little of their wood buildings, apart from post holes survived. It was only hordes of metal that survived, and occasionally horn and bone.

It had been a busy two weeks, and more evidence of some type of Saxon, possible burial had been discovered. Dr. Forster thought she now had enough evidence to put a funding bid together, which she would work on over the summer. Evan was still not sure he liked the idea of The Hill being dug into, but he had plenty of time to decide and make a final decision, if and when Dr. Forster received funding. Meanwhile he had plenty to keep himself busy.

The two families had moved out of Brynafon into the leased farm units at Manor Farm, the three houses opposite the school in Brynafon were now standing and should be fitted out by late August, and Evan himself still had to find another job.

He met up with Pete and Dave at the Dragon and Dagger at the end of the week. Ruby was up at the Manor Farm with Jed and Dr. Forster; the upcoming Rainbows Revival tour was imminent. Pete was looking decidedly happier than on their last meeting. Pete and Dave were sitting by the roaring open fire, which despite it being July, was needed for the unseasonal cold snap. The pub was full, everyone talking to friends and drowning their sorrows with a pint and bemoaning the turn in the weather. Pete was talking animatedly between mouthful of crisps.

"I think I've found her," he was saying to Dave when Evan arrived.

"Found who?" Asked Evan pulling up a seat by the fire.

"The girl for me," said Pete opening another bag of crisps and passing them round.

"Remember Agnes from school?" They did, Agnes had been rather plump and good at maths. She had been studious, and hadn't said much. She and her one friend, tall and lanky Catherine had stuck together tightly all through junior and secondary school. Catherine always came second in Maths. Agnes had been teased because of her plumpness, glasses and her academic ability. "Well, I bumped into her, literally, as it happens at the bank." Said Pete. "I was holding the door open for this lady coming out, when I was coming in, well she tripped, and fell into my arms! Well it was Agnes!"

"She was never much good at P.E always a bit clumsy, and always the last choice for netball and team games." Said Dave unimpressed.

"Well, she was carrying some books and things, so I helped pick them up for her, and when she stood up and said thanks, I realised who it was. Well, she's slim now, and no glasses, and actually quite attractive. Short dark hair, and dark eyes, she's got an amazing smile too. Anyway, she was a bit shy, but I asked if I could buy her lunch, once I finished my banking. It was rainy so I couldn't sit in the churchyard for my sandwiches which I usually do when it is fine, I just fancied some company, I don't have a lot in common with my work colleagues, they are mainly a lot older than I am and female. Well, we met in McDonalds, and we've kind of been meeting every lunchtime since. She works in the bank, she's the assistant manager, she's got a degree, and she's doing pretty well for herself."

Evan and Dave were impressed. Another round of drinks was called for. Perhaps Pete had heeded their talk after all a few weeks back.

"We just sit and talk, in the church yard, or at a coffee shop or fast food place. I hate my job in insurance, and she's been encouraging me to make a change, and perhaps get some more qualifications. You know, she's really interested in me, and what I'm doing! I'm even thinking of going into teacher training, I've always liked kids."

"Goodness!" Said Dave.

"Good for you," said Evan. "Maybe, this is the one – you never know mate, you never know!"

Chapter 18

Dr. Forster had gone back to her cottage outside Bristol to sort out her wet and muddy clothes and put the funding bid in. They would meet up with her again shortly in Bristol as Ruby and the Rainbow Revivals were playing festivals and venues in Cardiff, Liverpool and Bristol. There were two nights at each venue, and it looked incredibly hectic, if exciting, thought Ruby. Ruby had only been to one festival, and Evan had never been to any, so it would prove quite an experience for him. He had been hired by Jed that week as a roadie. He still had holiday time to take off work before the end of August.

"We could do with a pair of strong arms like you," Jed had said. "Nick and I aren't as young as we used to be, and can't carry what we used to. Nick's legs are bandy enough as it is!"

Evan was keen to oblige. Getting time off at the estate agency wasn't a problem as it would close at the end of next month anyway. He was also very relieved. He had hated the thought of Ruby going unbody guarded to the festivals, mainly because of her father still on the prowl. He knew Jed and Nick would take care of her, but they would be very busy, and he just wanted to be there, a pair of strong arms, as Jed had said.

Nick and Jed were taking equipment in the Rolls, and Evan's offer to help transport with the Land Rover was more than welcomed. Owain and Meg were on puppy looking after duties for the week, and Claire and Bronwyn were looking after Molly's kittens.

Jed had booked them all into a small hotel in Cardiff, they were to be joined by Benedict the violinist, and Deryn the harpist in Cardiff, although Deryn would not be on the rest of the tour having classical commitments of her own.

Ruby was more used to help organising archaeo-logical digs, but this seemed to need the same amount of organisation and preparation, if in a different way.

"At least we're not in a sea of mud in a windswept hillside in a tent," Said Ruby. In fact, the little hotel look-ing over the bay was rather pleasant, and the landlady attentative.

The festival was on a farm, "this is more like the windy, muddy hillsides I'm used to!" commented Ruby as they parked up to unload the gear. "Let's hope the weather is a bit better for the festival goers tonight!"

Evan was put to work immediately carting gear. Nick showed him what to do, and where to put everything, it appeared Nick had been a roadie as well as a chauffeur for Jed. The field area was massive, and Evan could see a multitude of brightly coloured tents on the horizon, people were arriving into the camping area in a steady stream, and he could see the steam rising from burger vans, and catering vans. On the artists side it was quieter, but only just, people scampered back and forward fetching and carrying. The first run through was a general run through, and Evan was able to sit back and enjoy the artists. They were all dressed casually in warm hoodies and fleeces, and they could have been anyone in the crowd, the costumes would be worn this evening. There were a real mix of styles, pop, rock, indie, heavy metal, country and everything in between, solo artists and bands. Most of the bands Evan hadn't heard of, he wasn't really into pop culture, but a few he had. He paid particular attention to the Revival's run through, the session musicians had arrived, it would be different ones, with different instruments at different venues. As far as Evan could tell, the Revivals session seemed to go fairly smoothly, Jed made a few changes, but kept them to a minimum. If Ruby was nervous, she didn't show it, she played harmoniously with Benedict, and she saw him giving her an encouraging thumbs up afterwards. Benedict was a real brick. After the rehearsal, Jed went over a few things with them, and then Ruby was free to go until the technical rehearsal that was later that morning. Evan thought it was as well that Jed was so experienced, unlike some of the groups where key people hadn't turned up, or they made a right hash of a number, Jed knew what he was doing.

Evan and Ruby decided to explore the audience compound, grabbing a coffee and croissant at one of the many catering vans. There were lots of stalls, selling food, clothes, camping supplies and wellingtons, CDs, gifts, crafts and services. Evan had not realised it would be so big or so commercial. It was colourful, noisy and teaming with life. There were marquees with activities for children and teenagers, yoga and drumming workshops, it seemed there was something for everyone. The rain was coming in showers still. At 12noon Evan checked his watch.

"Time to get going for the tech rehearsal," he said to Ruby. She nodded; she was indulging in a pink fluffy candy floss.

"Haven't had one of these since I was seven and we went to the beach!" Laughed Ruby, her head peeping out from Evan's old hoodie and a waterproof jacket.

The tech rehearsal was far less interesting thought Evan, as sound was balanced, instruments and amps adjusted, lighting flooded the stage in pools of coloured light. It was stop, start and eventually wound up at 1.30pm. The hotel was nearby so they spent a couple of hours eating and resting before getting back for 5p.m. Evan could see that touring and playing could be exhausting, in some ways it was similar to farming in that respect. He could see why Jed and his crew had burnt out; the pace was relentless.

Jed had a surprise for them, the album was out. His photograph of Ruby adorned the front cover, her red dress and pale skin showing well against the stone wall of the barn. Her black hair tossed to the wind, and her gaze smouldering, every bit the rock chick.

"It's already selling well, thank goodness!" Said Jed as they met for lunch at the hotel. "Copies are on sale at the festival, so that should be a boost to sales."

The evening went in a blur of sound and lights and action. The Rainbow Revivals were on a third of the way through, they appeared from a cloud of dry ice that engulfed the stage, it lit up to a backdrop of a rainbow with a pot of gold at the end of it. Jed strutted his stuff, his voice still good and powerful despite age. Ruby was placed on his right, in the front with Benedict on the other side near her, further back in the middle was

Deryn on the Welsh harp. The guitars and basses were off on the other side with the keyboard and the drums. Jed switched from guitar to keyboard and back again. Sometimes the other guitarists sung too. There was no doubt about it, Jed could still strut his stuff!

The whole thing was electrifying, riveting and dynamic, the sound and the lights and the costumes all came together in one glorious event. Evan found himself from his place backstage with Nick, clapping along, swaying with the beat, and to his surprise thoroughly enjoying himself. Yes, he thought, he could well see them attending a festival every year from now on.

The weather had brightened, the rain had stopped and later in the evening the stars came out. It was thought Evan, a magical event. The audience was enthusiastic, and clapped and swayed to the music. They were all ages, some older original Roaring Rainbows fans, delighted to see the reformed group. They often had families with teenage children with them. There were young children too, groups of teenagers and aging hippies. The whole world seemed to be there.

The man in the jeans, black T-shirt and green waterproof jacket, seemed to be enjoying himself like every other reveller. He was older, with white hair, and dark brown eyes, medium height, unremarkable, he could have been an original Roaring Rainbows fan. He held a can of lager in one hand, but if one had looked at him carefully, one would of realised he never drunk out of it. He was moving well, swaying in time with the music, although he hated this type of music, he preferred Wagner. He kept himself near a group of older Roaring Rainbows fans, but if one had observed him carefully, it would be observed he was not actually part of that group who had travelled on a coach together from Aberwysyth. He was on his own, he was Ruby's father.

Ruby, Evan, Jed, Nick and Benedict collapsed into their beds exhausted at one a.m. The day after next they had to leave at 9a.m. the next morning to make the long haul up to Liverpool.

"I think I'm too old for this!" Said Jed at breakfast. "If we ever do this again, I'll tell my agent that the venues need to be closer! Mind you, it was a big success, you should all be proud of yourself, and it should set us all up nicely. Ruby, my love, you were stunning, looked brilliant, and played brilliantly!" He blew a kiss across the breakfast table to Ruby, who giggled. Jed still had the charmer in him!

Benedict travelled north with Jed and Nick in the Rolls, which was more comfortable than Evan's Land Rover. The rainbow painted silver Rolls caused people to look and stare where ever they went.

"I'm just glad the old girl made it!" Said Nick quietly to Evan, referring to the Rolls when they reached Liverpool. "The old girls even more knackered than Jed and I, after this we should be able to get that Land Rover I've hankered after." Said Nick. Evan had got to know Nick a lot better on this trip. They were spending a lot of time together, roadieing and waiting patiently back stage. Evan liked Nick's quiet assured personality more and more, he was someone he trusted and respected, and like Owain he worked hard into his seventies. He deserved a break thought Evan.

There was another hotel in Liverpool, this time a ubiquitous cheap travel inn in the town centre. The venue this time was a concert hall, and it would just be the Rainbow Revivals. The agent had secured it last minute when the previous aging band's drummer had suddenly dropped dead at their last gig, and the band had decided to call it a day.

"I'm not sure we'll fill this one," Said Jed, when they arrived. "It's quite a big space. When we were the Roaring Rainbows, we filled Wembley, but now, who knows, but the Liverpudlians like their music, always give bands a warm welcome."

Evan found there were proper, if cramped dressing rooms, and the manager was obliging and helpful with all enquiries. Ruby and him were able to share a dressing room, although Evan had no dressing to do. Ruby, looked a bit more nervous this time, thought Evan, as she put her dark heavy make up on, red lip stick and slipped into the red dress and heels. But she didn't say anything, that was how Ruby handled pressure he'd learnt. She spent time meticulously tuning up her violin until she was happy with the result. Then she tuned up with Benedict, and finally with the rest of the band.

Evan had had a lot of time to think on the tour, he loved supporting Ruby, whether it was with her archaeology, the bakery or her music. But he didn't want to just support her, he wanted to provide for her and a family. Perhaps it was meeting his biological father that had made the difference, but he now knew, he wanted a family of his own. Ruby was young still, there was plenty of time, and he knew she loved children and animals too. He wanted to make a life for them with secure prospects and a future. He wanted that hill farm.

He would have another word with Owain to see if he had any bright ideas, and see when he secured another job if he could save up. It would be hard, of that he was sure, especially nowadays. A hill farm wouldn't bring in a lot he was sure, but they could diversify, run a holiday let, and perhaps Ruby would be able to lecture and write on archaeology, not just dig. That brought in a pittance. He had his share in the Brynafon Buy Out shop - his old estate agency shop, and he was going to increase that to a £1000 he had decided, that would make him a major shareholder. The café and bakery were going well, although in the Autumn there would no longer be the tourist trade passing through. Evan couldn't help it, like his mother he worried about the future, and in particular his and Ruby's future.

The Liverpool concert hall was three quarters full the first night, but it was a chance for the new band to run through all their new album in total, for the first time, and Jed threw in a few Roaring Rainbows classics just for good measure. Again, the audience was all ages, although more the older side, as some people had just transferred their tickets from the aging rock band that had been due to play there, and taken a punt on the Rainbow Revivals instead. They appeared to like what they heard and were enthusiastic in their applause.

Nick was out early and bought the local paper next day laying it out on the breakfast table triumphantly: "A thumpingly good, rip-roaring concert," he read out over the breakfast table. Ruby and Evan looked up from their toast and marmalade. "Some of the classic old Roaring Rainbows, with a Celtic and country new Rainbows Revival's twist. Sounds good, looks good and is good!"

"Well, that's better than I expected, reviewers can be the pits sometimes, that should fill the seats tonight." Jed said very pleased. He thumped his spoon on the table heartily, causing other guests to turn around.

Ruby and Evan had some down time that afternoon, Ruby did a little shopping for their new home above the bakery, and then they chilled out in the hotel pool. Having fun, splashing up and down and racing, Evan always won by a good amount.

"I could get used to this" Said Ruby. "Pity there's no pool in Brynafon or the New Town."

"We used to swim in the river when I was young," said Evan. "There's a spot where you can swim from the rocks at high tide, a little further down from where we crossed over when we crossed over in the inflatable, we could go there on a summer's evening." Said Evan.

"I'd like that very much," said Ruby giving him a kiss.

Although it was tiring Ruby found, playing a two-hour gig on their own in some ways it was more satisfying, they could step up the interaction between them. There was less faffing around with rehearsals, although the tech rehearsal took time, it was quicker than at the festival, where everything was very complicated. The concert hall was also satisfyingly full. The Liverpudlians, as Jed had said, were noisy and enthusiastic with their praise. Jed signed autographs backstage for ten minutes after they finished, and Ruby was asked to sign covers of the album and programme, mainly by the younger fans, she signed herself with the simple word "Red" and put in a heart and a kiss. On some she addressed it to the young person directly, to Liam or Lilly, or whoever it was.

Another day of travelling saw them reach Bristol and another festival venue. Apart from Benedict, they were staying in Dr. Forster's pretty cottage in a village on the outskirts of Bristol. Dr. Forster also had a room at the university where she often stayed when it was term time, but in the holidays, she was at her cottage. It was at the end of an unmade-up track, with views over hills and a field of cows lazily grazing. A small stone path under an arch lead to the red painted front door. There were two large bedrooms, Nick and Jed would stay in one, and Evan and Ruby would have the sofa bed in the lounge. But it was great to stay somewhere homely, with someone they knew. Dr. Forster had insisted and both Jed and Ruby were keen to accept. Ruby had stayed there before, Dr. Forster was quite sociable, and often had groups of her students staying, and barbecues in the pretty garden. It was an old brick-built cottage dating from around 1750 with large classical Georgian windows that let in plenty of light, and a sloping low roof, ending in a cat slide roof on the left. There was a kitchen and cosy sitting room downstairs, and meals were taken round the farmhouse table. There was also a handy utility room, which according to Dr. Forster had once been a little dairy attached to the house. This had a large butler's sink in and trestle type table, where Dr. Forster cleaned and sorted her finds, and had plenty of hanging space for wet clothes and storage for muddy boots.

"Most useful," Said Dr. Forster as she greeted them warmly. " That's one of the reasons I bought the place. It was pretty derelict when I first came here twenty years ago, it was owned by an old lady who had died. But apart from putting in a wood burner that heats the house and the water, I haven't done much to the place, just stripped back the wall paper to reveal lovely fireplaces in each room, and got the place woodworm and damp treated really."

She showed them outside, there was a ramshackled wooden shed for her car, another for her tools. "I have a gardener in once a week, he's wonderful. I don't have much time for gardening, but he cuts the grass and grows me the most wonderful vegetables, here I'll show you."

She showed them a wonderful array of runner beans propped up on A frame poles, tomatoes and beds of vegetable growing.

"I like to each healthily and organically," she said. "None of that chemical rubbish in my food. I belong to the Soil Association which is handily based in Bristol."

The rest of the garden was an orchard, with plums, cherries, apples and pears growing in profusion, and wild flowers between the long grass in the orchard meadow. There was also a clay oven that Dr. Forster and the students had made, a fire pit, well used, with logs for sitting in it around it, and a primitive clay kiln for bakery pottery, another archaeology experiment. Various wattle huts stood around in various states of decay, one was covered with turfs, and another had what looked like an old goat's skin on it.

"Experiments in Mesolithic temporary dwellings," indicated Dr. Forster. "I think some students would have survived better in the Mesolithic than others!" She smiled.

"I used to love it when Dr. Forster invited us here!" Said Ruby, she was positively dragging Evan by the hand round the garden, and skipping for joy as she came across various features she recognised. Evan could see why, he would love a place like this for him and Ruby, and the little children and animals running around.

"It's wonderful," said Evan. "Thank you so much for inviting us!"

"Well, I wasn't going to miss this opportunity of having you here, was I!" Beamed Dr. Forster.

Jed was looking extremely happy too, and Nick very relaxed. A tabby cat slunk through the grass, and rubbed herself up against Nick.

"Oh, that's Bartholomew, he's not mine, he comes over from the next cottage, he likes to hunt here, and make himself at home." Said Dr. Forster.

The inside of Dr. Forster's house was simply attired, there were a couple of old sofas covered in throws of Indian cotton in pink and orange. There was her work desk, a rather nice old Georgian writing desk by the window over-looking the orchard. A dark wood circular small table stood behind it with a lamp and her hand axe on it, it was acting as a paper weight for a pile of papers. The main feature of the room was a hand-made pine bookcase that took up all one wall, apart from the middle section, where there was a door leading up to the bedrooms and bathroom. The book case was stuffed full of books and journals to overflowing. They piled up on the floor around it. Clearly Dr. Forster was very well read, and her research materials were impressive.

Dinner was a hearty beef, bean and apple stew, followed by a large bowl of fruit from the garden. There were bottles of apple cider made locally, apple juice from the garden and red and white wine. Dr. Forster was nothing if not generous in her hospitality.

"This is delicious!" Said Evan appreciatively. "So much better than the hotel food we had last night."

"I'm glad," replied Dr. Forster. "It's all local and organic, and most of the vegetables, fruit and herbs come from my garden. The cider orchard is only three miles away too!"

Jed looked suitably impressed.

"I've got tickets for both nights of your performances at the festival." Dr. Forster was saying.

"Oh, we didn't expect you to come both nights!" Exclaimed Jed. "I'll make sure you get a backstage pass to see us."

"Oh, it's my pleasure," said Dr. Forster. "It's quite a few years ago that I went to a festival, I can tell you. I contacted a few students and ex-students over social media, I knew quite a few would be going, and they've kindly invited me to join their groups both nights, so I won't be bopping on my own!" She laughed.

Evan smiled; Dr. Forster was as up for fun as usual. The middle aged bespeckled exterior hid a young enthusiastic girl at heart still.

They were up and out again for 9a.m. the next day. They found a note on the table, eggs from the next cottage were out, plus a note that honey cured bacon was in the fridge. There was also a large artisan loaf that Ruby approved of, home-made jam from a neighbour and tea and coffee. They helped themselves. Ruby espied Dr. Forster in the orchard, she was taking delivery of a hive of bees for a neighbour, plus a coop of colourful hens, mainly Marans had arrived from the same neighbour to forage in the orchard. The neighbour would be looking after both the bees and hens.

"Free, free range eggs!" Dr. Forster had said, "plus I hope to acquire some honey and also have a shot at making honey mead with the students, all in the name of historical authentic research of course!"

Ruby laughed.

"Oh, I have something for you, Ruby." Said Dr. Forster when she came back inside. She rummaged in a cupboard and came out with a Bristol University hoodie. "One of my departing students gave me this, never worn. I thought you might be able to blend in with crowd a bit in this if you are out in the city. Although it's holidays, they'll be plenty of University hoodies around the city, quite a few of my students are local, and a lot stay here in the summer to find work, especially if they come from high unemployment areas."

"Thank you," said Ruby taking it gratefully.

"See you at the festival, then!" Said Dr. Forster as they departed out the door.

The sun was already getting up heat, and it looked like the weekend would be one of good weather. The venue was again another farm, and Ruby and Evan were getting used to the procedures now, it was all becoming more familiar. This time they were three quarter ways through the line-up, the festival, if anything was even bigger than Cardiff. The Rainbow Revivals also had a longer slot and were show casing more of their songs. The Friday evening was glorious. Smoke drifted in plumes straight upwards from the many barbecues in the audience and people laughed, sang, played the guitars and generally were in high spirits before the event started in the evening. Again, the Rainbow Revivals went down well, and the music press wanted to interview Jed about his new-found style and his creativity, and what it was like to be back touring again. A fashion magazine wanted a photograph of Ruby in her red dress for their front cover, and she obliged. She was as uncommital as possible for the short interview afterwards with them. Fortunately, the magazine seemed more concerned with the trivia of her hair, makeup and dress than it was about her life. All she really said about herself was that she had started playing violin at six years old. That all suited Ruby well. She was only referred to by her stage name "Red".

Ruby and Evan spent the next day with Dr. Forster, she wanted to show them a dig by Severn which had unearthed Mesolithic remains, including wonderful footprints in the mud, and the remains of a temporary hearth. They also went to a mock-up of an iron age village, complete with thatched huts, and Iron Age type pigs. Evan was most interested in the pigs and Soay and Hebridean sheep they had representing the type of animal available in the Iron Age. The Soay and Hebrideans' shed their own fleeces, were wild and flighty and came in a lovely warm beige colour and darker brown, which looked most attractive. Evan decided this was one of the ways he was going to go with his sheep herds. Coloured, natural wools for spinning and weaving. He could add Jacob's with their multi coloured fleeces and Manx Langhorns to his flocks too.

On Saturday there were two performances, one in the afternoon, slightly shorter and more family orientated and one in the evening with laser light displays and fireworks. It was exhausting but exhilarating, the hot weather became even hotter, ending in a spectacular thunder storm as the evening ended. People exiting ran for shelter, and hurriedly put up umbrellas.

It was two a.m. by the time they arrived back at Dr. Forster's. They were going to have a relaxed morning there and Sunday lunch before going home.

"I'm not sure how I'm going to make work on Monday morning!" Yawned Ruby as she snuggled into Evan on the way back to Dr. Forster's. They were all in the Rolls, Jed was asleep in the front passenger seat.

Interesting enough when everyone finally emerged at 12 noon the next day, Nick said Jed's bed was unslept in. Ruby gave Evan a conspiratorial nudge in the ribs. While Dr. Forster was making lunch, she called Ruby over to help her. She turned to Ruby in a hushed voice.

"Ruby," she said. "I need to run something past you, well, it's all a bit new to me, it's normally me giving advice to lovelorn students, not the other way around!"

Ruby's eyes widened, but she didn't say anything, as Dr. Foster passed her the cabbage to chop up.

"It's Jed," said Dr. Foster, she looked slightly embarrassed. "He's asked me to move in with him at Manor Farm! But, I'm not sure. I like him, of course I do, he's different to anyone I've ever met, and he's caring." She paused.

Jed was certainly different thought, Ruby. She could imagine Dr. Forster had not met anyone like him before.

"He's witty, and fun and wonderfully talented of course!" Continued Dr. Forster, "and I'm honoured..... but he's twenty years older than me, and I'm, well, quite set in my ways and happy with my life. I like my cottage; I've got a good job lecturing and writing. Oh, I've thought about giving up lecturing now everything is so pressurised and cost cutting nowadays, but what would

I do? I'm too old to dig day in and day out, beside that doesn't pay the bills."

Dr. Forster was nothing but practical.

Ruby considered carefully.

"I'd think about it a bit," she said wisely. "This is all quite sudden really. You can always stay with Jed in the holidays, and come back here in term times, can't you?"

Dr. Forster nodded, and absent mindedly started peeling the carrots into the sink. "I wasn't thinking of retiring till sixty, that's a few years yet. I'm supervising a dig in the Orkneys for the next two weeks anyway…. yes, you're right. I'm not sure I want to change everything. I'll go on the dig, come back here, he can always visit if he wants to, then I'll go to Brynafon again at the end of the holidays after I've put in the funding bid." Dr. Forster nodded to herself.

"Do you think, he'll be disappointed?" She asked anxiously.

"I think he'll be happy you'll visit him again at the end of the holidays," said Ruby. "There's no need to rush things, is there?"

Dr. Forster smiled. "Thank you, Ruby." She said. "It's good to have a younger perspective on things sometimes."

If Jed was disappointed in Dr. Forster's answer, he kept it to himself. They had a splendid meal of roast beef and potatoes from the garden, followed by a rubbard pie with thick cream and custard. Dr. Forster loaded Ruby with books from her splendid collection that she thought she might like to read, saying she would pick them up at the end of the holidays from her.

Ruby thanked her kindly, and gave her a big hug, She, for one was glad that she would be seeing Dr. Forster again over the summer.

Dr. Forster left the next day for the Orkneys, flying first from Bristol to Aberdeen and then getting another plane out to the islands. Her mind firmly on the dig and her commitments, she had been looking forward to this dig all year, there were amazing Neolithic remains in the Orkneys, and she hoped to get time to see them all. It was therefore a surprise that the next day she received a phone call from the policed in Bristol - her cottage had been broken into. The neighbour with the chickens and beehives had found the front door slightly ajar when he came around to check his flock. Nothing as far as he could tell was missing. Papers had been strewn around from her desk, and some of the books had been pulled out of the bookcase, nothing looked like it had been touched upstairs thank goodness.

"Do you have your lap top with you?" Asked the police. It was the only thing the neighbour said might be missing.

"Yes," she replied, "It's here with me."

"It looks like the intruder was looking for something. Do you have anything or value in the house?"

Dr. Forster didn't, she had one pearl necklace from her grandmother, and the police checked that was still in her jewellery box, which also housed, oddly for them, a lot of flint chippings.

The police had secured the house, they were at a loss as to why it had been burgled. Perhaps the burglar had been disturbed and left? They posited.

Dr. Forster shuddered, even in the gale that was blowing across the Orkneys. She had a very good idea who it was, and what he was after. It had to be Ruby's father, and he was after any information on her laptop that showed information and correspondence with Ruby. She had deleted it all of course, but she knew it was still there somewhere in the system. Thank goodness, she had it with her.

She called her gardener and neighbour to check the place daily for her, and she upped the gardener's visit to daily while she was away. Then she left a message on Bill Clackett's office phone, it simply said: "He was at my cottage."

A week later both Bill Clackett's Estate Agency and home were broken into, computers hacked into and papers strewn around again nothing was taken. Ruby's Dad was closing the net.

Chapter 19

Life went back to normal. Ruby returned very sleepily to the bakery, and Evan to his job at the Estate Agency. It was the school summer holidays, and tourists came in greater numbers than ever to Brynafon, and on good days the bakery café was packed. It seemed the word had got out that this was a good venue at the end of a walk or cycle ride. Apparently, some trendy person had put it on social media, said Ruby, and a lot of their friends had decided to come and give it a try, and obviously liked what they saw. Tourist gifts of Welsh blankets, cushions, and craft made items were all selling well. In winter, it would be quite different, thought Ruby. The bunting that had been made for Ruby and Evan's wedding, stayed up, fluttering colourfully in the breeze, giving the place a celebratory air.

Other small changes were happing too. Nick had sold the rainbow painted Rolls at last, and had bought a Land Rover.

"I should have done it earlier," he confessed to Evan, when they met for lunch one day at the café. "It was Dave that helped, when I asked him to sell it for me, he said I should auction it on a website. So, he put it on one for me, and guess what there were lots of old Roaring

Rainbows fans bidding for it. It made £60,000! That old bit of clapped out metal! I would have done it earlier if I'd known, but I suppose I couldn't have. The Rainbows Revivals has re-launched interest in the original Roaring Rainbows, and old albums are selling again, and memorabilia, fancy that after all these years!" Nick couldn't quite believe his luck.

Evan had also been keeping Dave busy. He'd asked Dave to spray out the "Bill Clackett Estate Agent" sign on the sides of the Land Rover. It was now a uniform green. Bill Clackett didn't need to advertise his Estate Agency business anymore.

Ruby had received her exam results back; she had received a first-class pass. She had jumped up and down on the bed for a good five minutes when she had received the news. Evan was pleased he'd made a good job of building the bed strongly! Evan was so proud of her. It hadn't been easy for her having to leave her course in January. But Ruby had worked hard, and with Dr. Forster's guidance, hadn't just succeeded, but had succeeded with flying colours.

There was other good news to, Evan's mum and Clive had become engaged, and the wedding was fixed for mid-August, the reception would be held at the café again, the wedding itself would take place at the chapel with the pastor presiding. Evan's mum was positively beaming when she told Evan and Ruby the news over Sunday lunch. Evan couldn't have been happier for her, and he gave his Mum the biggest of hugs. He was to give his mum away, and Ruby and Mary would be matrons of honour. It was just going to be a small wedding. Clive didn't have any family, and they wanted something small and intimate. Clive had splashed out on a honeymoon for a week in Corfu for them, Evan's mum had never been abroad, and she was very excited. She asked Ruby advice over lunch about what she should wear, and Ruby advised her that the sales of summer clothing would be on soon. Evan's mum was positively giggly like a school girl again, and Evan caught a rare sight of the 16-year-old fresh face girl that had once enticed Clive in his youth. Rather than the care worn and hard-working mother who he usually saw. He and his mother had applied for passports at the same time, both had never had need of them before. He felt with Ruby it was a wise precaution, you never knew with Ruby what twist her life would take next!

"I'll buy your going away dress, Mum!" Said Evan. "I think we'll need Ruby's help in deciding." He turned to Ruby who was nodding enthusiastically. The women were going to hit the sales.

Dave and Sian had also decided getting married over the August bank holiday weekend. It would be a month of celebrations. The pastor had never known so many weddings in Brynafon in August, any plans for a holiday were firmly scuppered until September. He didn't mind, he was pleased his little chapel would host so many marriages, and anyway a holiday in September would be better for his bank balance.

The houses opposite the school had been completed and three families from the village had moved in there. Dave and Sian were now due to buy one of the vacated terrace cottages, as a previous sale had fallen through.

The only cloud on the horizon, was for Evan his looming unemployment. He tried not to let it show, or get him down, but it hung there like a low black cloud, refusing to go away.

He'd seen Owain as soon as he'd got back, he'd had Clive check on him daily when he had been away. Owain, was looking tired and he had a cough, and Evan felt guilty landing him and Meg with the pups. Owain and Meg were both glad to hand Beth and Bruce back to their owners.

"Reckon we're too old for another pup," said Owain glancing down at Meg who was sound asleep at his feet. The house looked chaos. Evan said he would spend every evening that week tidying, cleaning and mending the puppy damage.

"Sorry, Owain," he said.

"Oh, it's OK boy, the pups had a whale of a time, and I didn't mind them really. You couldn't leave Ruby unprotected could you?" Said Owain. "Now tell me about the trip, I expect I'll hear all from Jed too." Owain quite liked to hear a bit of gossip.

Evan smiled, and told him the details. He purposely left out Jed's offer and solicitations to Dr. Forster. If Jed wanted that known, he could tell his friend Owain himself.

Evan and Ruby came and cleaned, tidied and repaired Owain's house for an hour every evening. He took the opportunity to thrash through more ideas about his ambition to be a hill farmer with Owain.

"Look," said Owain at the end of the week. "I'm not getting any younger, and I don't know what it is, but I've just not been feeling right for a month now. I could do with the extra help, and I worry if I'm ill, what will happen to the farm and the animals? Why don't we share the farm? Half the profits?"

Evan stood thinking, it was no doubt generous of Owain. But there was hardly enough for Owain to live on, let alone survive on half of that. He thought for a while, pacing the room.

"Sit down, boy!" Commanded Owain beckoning to the other worn out chair by the hearth. "You're making me tired just looking at you!"

"Thanks," he said at last. Owain was puffing on his pipe, his eyes now half closed, as he sat in the front room, Meg at his feet with her paws crossed. "I'd like that," continued Evan "but I don't want half the profits, that doesn't leave you enough. No, I've been thinking, if I can just build up the flock in a few different ways, if I make any money out of my small flock and any additions I make, I'll just keep that. I'll still have to get another job, perhaps for a year anyway."

"As you wish." Said Owain, he closed his eyes and started to snore.

There was some other good news as well for Ruby. Two weeks after they had come back from touring, Jed presented her with a cheque at the café, grinning madly.

"Nick's done the accounting, as this is your share from the concerts."

Ruby took it, her eyes widened when she saw the amount. "Are you sure, Jed?" She said.

It was enough to buy half the bakery.

"You earned it," said Jed with a grin. "We've even been booked by Cardiff for next year!"

Ruby gave him a kiss on the cheek, this was really all his doing. The next day she put money into savings that would pay for half of the bakery. Evan kept his week's wages for roadieing to tide him over in September, it was all welcome.

Two weeks later Ruby found a royalty payment from the album had been deposited in her bank, it was more than enough to pay for the rest of the bakery. Ruby was amazed, in her wildest dreams she had not imagined such good fortune.

"I'm not sure I like being a kept man," said Evan as he and Ruby snuggled in bed on Sunday morning. He was glad to be back in their own bed, in their own little place after the exhausting touring.

"Get used to it, but after this it's up to you! Besides," Said Ruby propping herself up on one arm and kissing him. "You took me on when I was a nothing down and out, with nothing with a reputation of a local whore! You took a chance on me, you've got to accept the smooth with the rough you know." She took her pillow and playfully hit him with it. He grabbed her and the pillow and turned her over.

"As long as I get my marital fill!" He said smiling.

As things turned out they fortuously moved into the rooms above the bakery slightly earlier than planned because of the lack of mortgage. The purchase had been blessedly straight forward, in Evan's books that in itself nowadays was rare enough. That Sunday they carted what few possessions they had into the upper rooms and kitchen. Evan had a wonderful surprise for Ruby too. Not only had he made a fine pine wooden bed for them taking the mattress from the shepherd's hut, but he had made a splendid Welsh dresser. Pete helped him carry it indoors, and place it in the kitchen. They all stood back admiring it, it looked just right there.

Ruby's eyes were wide with disbelief and pleasure: "Evan, you're amazing!" She said giving him a big kiss and hug. "I'll have to get some nice china at some point to show it off!"

"I've been making it in Owain's barn when you were studying," said Evan pleased at her reaction.

"But it's so good, Evan. You could do carpentry professionally, look at those joints, amazing!"

"I studied one of Jed's old pieces," said Evan. "It was a bit of trial and error, but I got there in the end, this is my rather late wedding present to you!"

"It's wonderful!" Said Ruby again. It looked at home in the bakery kitchen, and meant they had a somewhere to keep their things, as well as the commercial bakery area.

The back bedroom was still full of gear to be sorted, so the first night they slept in the bigger front bedroom that would be their lounge. Ruby slept soundly, she found all the heavy lifting hard work. He looked at her pale skin on the pillow, and red mouth and black glossy hair. He couldn't sleep, there was a lot happening and his mind was turning over. He had been roused abruptly from sleep by an old childhood nightmare of his dad dragging him off The Hill. The beads of sweat still hung on him, he wiped his face on his T-shirt, and pulled another from the top of a box in the corner. Putting it on, he went to the window, pulling the curtains back a little. There was a full moon, the nightmare generally occurred on a full moon he had found. When as a child, he had liked to be on The Hill the most, with the moon rising above The Hill, its ghostly form and light bringing a special primaeval almost spiritual feeling to The Hill. He sighed deeply, things were better now, so much better than those early years, they had a place to call home, he owned The Hill and most of all, he had Ruby as his wife.

Chapter 20

It was the last week in August. His mother and Clive had been wed at the chapel and were off on honeymoon in Corfu. As it happened Jed was also away, he had taken Dr. Forster for a week in Turkey, it was somewhat of a compromise for both of them, but they were both looking forward to it greatly, and who knows, they might work something out.

Dave and Sian had also been married, unlike the rather quiet affair of his mother and Clive, Dave had hired Jed, Ruby and Benedict to play for them, and there had been dancing at the café until the early hours. They had also booked out the Dragon and Dagger for a meal for thirty guests, including Evan and Ruby, the pub was as full as it had ever been. The young married couple had gone to the Pembroke coast for a week afterwards, after that they were holed up in a room behind the garage until they could secure better marital accommodation in the village, their offer for the terrace cottage having only just been accepted. Evan supposed the room behind the garage was slightly less cramped than the shepherd's hut. Dave had also just purchased the garage from his boss who had also retired suddenly after he had unfortunately had a stroke. He'd secured it at a good price, and had ideas for it, it was doing fine as it was, but Dave was thinking of taking a course in forging iron, and running a forge from there as well.

"It's all there," he said to Evan at the pub, when he met with Pete for their weekly boys' night out. "It was a forge before it was a garage, and all the equipment is still there. It'll need updating of course. But Ruby putting the bakery back into action made me think. Why should we have to go all the way into the New Town to get a bit of metal work fixed? The farmers are always asking me can I weld this or that for them, why don't we offer the service here in Brynafon? I can even take a farrier's course and start to shoe the local horses. Save Clare and Bronwyn a fortune.

Evan nodded, it made sense. Pete had news too, he and Agnes were having a week in Spain together, things were going along so well, and he had been accepted for teacher training in Cardiff.

"It'll mean me staying away during the week," he said, "and of course there won't be money coming in, so Agnes and I thought we'd make the most of it and have a holiday in early September before I start."

Evan nodded, he was pleased for Pete, and he bought another round to celebrate, but it seemed everyone had a future but him. A week to go, and still no work. He drank his coke quietly in a thoughtful mood.

It was in that last week of August that Evan finally landed a job. It was not great, but it would do. It didn't pay as much as the estate agents, but he hoped it wouldn't be for more than a year. He found it, much as he had his estate agency job, walking along from Bill Clackett's, where he had been helping Bill sort out some of the paperwork. It was at the cheaper end of town and was at a yard which supplied animal feed stuff, mainly by delivery to outlying farms. The good thing about it was that he was not going to be stuck in an office in the New Town. The rather scruffy notice was pinned to the wooden gate, which was equally as scruffy read: "Driver required, must know the area, Monday to Friday" and that was it.

It was a small firm with an absent owner. Evan climbed up the Victorian iron stairs at the front of the building to the one small rather tatty office. The foreman was a big rough looking man with dark hair in his late forties wearing a red and white checked shirt, braces and dirty jeans. There were three other people in the office, an officious looking prim lady in her late fifties with dark hair in a bun, in a tidy, if well worn, blue skirt and jacket, a young girl with blonde curls who looked about eighteen, in a flowery summer dress. He learnt that Ada, the older lady was in charge of the accounts, payroll and admin, and Gwynne helped her. There was a lad about eighteen as well, skinny and tall with sandy coloured hair. He served the customers that came direct to the warehouse, and helped load the van in the morning.

"You got a clean licence?" The foreman asked Evan, assessing him up and down. "Look like you're strong enough to do the job. Last guy had a heart attack on the job a week ago, damned inconvenient, got all this feed to get out. You have to navigate you know, can't just rely on a Satnav to find the farms."

"I can read ordnance survey maps." Said Evan.

There was a pause, while the boss, who he learnt was Ivor lit up.

"When can you start, then?" He asked.

"Next Tuesday," replied Evan, and that was that. He wasn't asked for his licence, or shown over the van.

"We start at 8a.m. finish at 4p.m." Said Ivor, and that was clearly as much information that Evan was going to get.

It was a wrench for Evan leaving his little office at Brynafon, a big wrench, that was for sure. But Evan was pleased to know he would still have a stake in the future there, as he handed the keys to the Brynafon Buy Out team on his last day. It was even worse saying goodbye to Bill Clackett.

"You and Ruby are coming over regularly for Sunday, lunch you know." Said Bill giving Evan a hug. "You're family to me, like a son you know. I want to hear regularly how you are both doing." Evan nodded, it was all he could do to stop the tears flowing.

He turned up smartly at 7.50a.m.on the Tuesday after the August bank holiday for his new job. It made for a very early start with the animals at Owain's farm, and it was going to be very difficult in the winter, especially when the road to Brynafon was covered in snow and ice.

Ada was already in, as was Eldon loading the van. He said good morning to Eldon briefly before seeing Ada. He was relieved when she asked to photocopy his driving licence and took his bank details for his pay.

"You can grab a quick cuppa before you go," she said. She indicated to the kettle. Evan declined but thanked her. Ada seemed a bit grim, but she efficient and thoughtful. Both Gwynne and Ivor turned up at 8a.m. By that time Eldon had finished loading, and was running through the list of calls with Evan. He gave him some pointers on difficult to find places. "There's mobile numbers," he said, "but often as not no reception, and watch the sheep dog at Bank Farm – it bites."

Ivor said nothing, but scowled at him and Eldon, Eldon slunk away, he had clearly said too much. Evan was relieved when he pulled out of the gates promptly at 8a.m. The van was slow and heavy, the brakes were worn, one of the brake lights didn't work. He'd have a word about that, and the van was dirty, covered in cigarette ash. It appeared he had a different patch to work every day. Today he was south east towards Chepstow, the next day he was south and west, after that it was west into the mountains, and on Thursdays he was at Brynafon and the surrounding farms. He went further north over the mountains again on the Friday. He had to be careful with the van, it was decidedly ropey. But he was glad to be out and about, and away from the yard and Ivor. His first day went relatively well, he took notes, marked on the ordnance survey maps where he had found the hard to find farms, and taken photos of landmarks to help him locate them. He only had to phone once, and here he had mobile reception. It was a beautiful day, and there was a lot of feed to be delivered to racehorses round Chepstow, despite it all, he found he was enjoying his job. The yard staff he met were pleased to see him, and passed the time of day. They often knew where the next racing yard or farm was on his route, he soon found and were willing to give him directions.

"You're an improvement on the last chap," he had said to him at half a dozen places. "He was late, rude, uncouth, swore and never stubbed his cigarettes out, it's no smoking here."

At first Evan thought they were just being polite, particularly a rather lovely blonde young lady at one racing stables, but he soon learnt, he couldn't have done much worse than his predecessor. With all the stopping to find the yards Evan was late back arriving at 4.15pm. Everyone had gone home except Ada, who he handed the keys back to.

"How did you get?" She enquired.

"Well," said Evan.

"Couldn't be any worse than Liam, lazy, uncouth bugger." Said Ada with feeling. Evan smiled; he was beginning to warm to Ada.

The second day he was in the south, there was more a range of business to be supplied here. Riding schools, chicken farms, private individuals, a few farms and commercial outlets.

It was a real mixture, and again there were no real problems. He had left a note for Ivor about the non-working brake light but he'd had no reply. He soon learnt that Ivor never bothered to ring or check on him, it was a relief. The further west and north he went the more rugged the terrain became and the van barely made it up the hills. The farms here were more isolated and he was in some of his favourite hill farming country. It was predominately livestock feed here, and he found him invited in for a cuppa at a few of the farms, it was a good opportunity to learn about hill farming from someone other than Owain. He looked at cattle herds, upland sheep and even a field of alpacas.

"Worth a lot, compared with a sheep, you can get ten times as much for their fleece, believe me alpacas are the way to go!" Said the proud owner, a lady who had moved to Wales and branched into alpacas some years back. Evan made note, alpacas needed more looking after, but they just might be worth the extra trouble. He was also able to see her flock of rare breed sheep. Everything on her small holding was in excellent health and condition.

"Could you sell me some?" He asked hopefully.

"I would think so." Said the farmer. Evan had just found his source of good breeding animals.

His best day though was a Thursday, when he mana-ged to re-arrange his route so that he could have lunch with Ruby at the café. It was also his shortest day work wise, so he could manage a good three quarters of an hour with her.

The weeks passed by. Ivor didn't get the brake light fixed, on the second week Evan secured the part from Dave and fixed it himself in his lunch break. He had also given the van a through clean, inside and out.

It wasn't all work though, and finishing at 4p.m. meant he was home soon after Ruby finished. There had been a new arrival in Evan's family, Molly's black and white kitten named Cleo was now ensconced in the bakery. It was popular with all the visitors, and Cleo and Beth the puppy played madly, it was exhausting, if pleasurable for Ruby. Ruby had been excepted to do a part time Masters with Dr. Forster at Bristol, it would mean her being away perhaps part of the week. Evan was nervous about it; her father was still on the loose. But he tried not to dampen her enthusiasm. Ruby would be cutting down her time serving at the café, and con-centrating on doing the accounts and admin, plus stu-dying for her Masters. She was already beginning to read the books Dr. Forster had given her. She had not wasted time, she had already put in ideas for her book on the archaeology of that part of Wales with some academic publishers. Dr. Forster's publisher was making encouraging noises about it.

Evan had not been slow off the mark either, he had secured some native breed sheep from the small holder on his rounds. These would be arriving shortly, the more expensive alpacas would probably have to wait until the Spring, Evan spent his summer evenings making separate enclosures for them.

"They're different." Said Owain, puffing on his pipe as he surveyed them on a lovely summer evening in the paddock. "Wild looking things, like deer, jump like deer too, nice coats though, and easy to look after, what with no sheering. We'll just have to wait and see how they do."

Owain looked at them contentedly, he was secretly pleased with Evan's purchases, he wished him every success. He glanced down at Meg at his side:

"I reckon you'll have your work cut out herding that lot," he said to her. Meg picked up her ears as if she had understood every word he was saying. "Wild looking bunch they are, guess that's why they are known as a primitive breed!" He tickled Meg behind her ears.

He was looking a little bit more rested now that Evan was doing half the work load, colour had returned to his cheeks a little, although he was still very gaunt.

"Reckon it's nice Meg," he said to her again between puffs on his pipe, "just to enjoy our flocks, and let some-one else get on with all the hard work!" Meg lay down and put her head on her paws contentedly.

Evan was busy in these light evenings, he had started on Beth the puppy's training. It helped having Owain and Meg to guide them both. He felt they were both making good progress.

Ruby had also had a few new ideas for the café, she had taken photographs of the landscape in and around

Brynafon and when they were on honeymoon in the Priory valley. These she had placed on the walls in the café. Not only did they brighten the place up, but they were all for sale, and some had sold to tourists already. One of the young mums in the village was an aspiring artist and her paintings of local animals and landscapes also adorned the walls.

Ruby took a commission each time a sale was made. The native and primitive breed sheep proved a good subject matter, and were an attraction for tourists and the school children alike. Ruby had also displayed photographs of the finds from the dig at the Hill, and some of the finds themselves that had now come back from the primary school. These nestled in one corner, and supplied a talking point for locals and tourists alike.

Ruby had also had a visitor, and Evan had to admit, for the first time in his life he had slight pangs of jealousy. The curator, Christian, from the New Town museum had come to see Ruby, to run over some ideas about the new display for The Hill finds that was developing all the time. Christian was young, tall, lanky and geeky with unruly blonde curls and glasses. He thought, Evan, was the type of guy Ruby should have married. They certainly seemed deep in conversation that Thursday lunch time at the café, when Evan joined them. He pushed his jealous thoughts to one side, and sat down.

"The display at the museum is proving really popular with school children," said Ruby brightly clasping Evan's hand. "Christian's even thinking of making a mini mound of The Hill in paper mache, with help from the New Town secondary school."

Evan smiled. "Great!" He said.

Ruby showed Christian the little exhibition she had made herself at the bakery café, then they chatted some more about The Hill, the recent excavations, Dr. Forster's funding bid and Ruby's Master's degree. Evan tried to keep up.

When Christian had left, Ruby clasped both his hands and gave him a kiss, she knew what he was thinking.

"Evan," she said. "It's you I love and married. If I'd have wanted a chap like Christian, I could have had half a dozen or so of those at University! I wanted you!"

Evan looked a little ashamed. "I couldn't help it," he said. "I just saw you together, and you're part of the same world."

"And now I'm part of your world, and loving our increasing role in hill farming, I wouldn't change anything Evan!"

She gave him a big kiss, she knew things were hard for him at the moment, the job change to a less good job, the lack of prospects in hill farming, and her being the one who purchased the bakery. Evan liked things to run fairly smoothly and predictably, but life wasn't like that sometimes, she was able to make the changes, possibly thanks to her army childhood, for Evan it was more difficult.

"I suppose," said Evan. "I just can't believe what a lucky bloke I am having you!"

Ruby kissed him again.

Chapter 21

As it was Evan's job did not last much more than a month. Evan now had the deliveries going quite smoothly, and he was well liked by his clients on his rounds. If word had got back to Ivor about his success, Ivor had yet to acknowledge it. But Ada had indicated that clients putting in their orders had been delighted by their new driver. Evan was pleased, he liked to make a good impression. He was enjoying the job, even though living on a basic wage was quite a challenge. The van was getting even slower, and Evan had had to tape on the driver's side mirror when it dropped off, it remained taped up. He had informed Ivor that it was very unlikely to pass its next MOT and the brakes were positively hazardous. Ivor had grunted – and done nothing.

It was early September, a fine morning, when Evan came in and looked at the list for the week Eldon had supplied him with. He frowned, there was a new customer, and the postcode could not possibly be right. He called Eldon over, but he did not know, that's what he had been given by Gwynne. Evan decided he better quickly sort it out for himself, he'd get Ada to double check. He bounded up the stairs two at a time, this delay would hold him up. The office was empty, he frowned, he knew everyone was in. He could hear the kettle brewing, probably Ada was with it making a cuppa for her boss. He was just about to enter the small cupboard space that doubled as a kitchen, when he heard a noise. There it was again, it was like a whimper, and then there was a clear: "No, please don't!" It was Gwynne's voice, she sounded terrified. He ran towards the noise which was coming from the stationery cupboard which was at the other end of the building. In a few bounding paces he was there, he threw open the door, he stopped in shock for a second.

Gwynne was pressed against the door by Ivor, her blouse was open, and Ivor's rough hands were down her bra, his other hand was up her skirt. The poor girl was whimpering and sobbing.

"Get off her!" Shouted Evan, he grabbed hold of Ivor and pulled him backwards off the girl, who tried to make a dash for the door, Ivor's big rough arm grabbed her and threw her back against the wall, her head impacting on it with a thud. She yelled loudly.

"Mind yer own fucking business, get out or you're fired!"

Evan saw red, this is what it must have been like for his beloved Ruby. Ivor put his hand in his trousers to get his appendage out. Evan grabbed him again, and swung him round.

"You're fired, get out!" Shouted Ivor. Gwynne darted for the door again, Ivor reached out for her again. Evan's right hook connected with Ivor's jaw and he went down like a stone. Evan could hear his jaw shattering. He turned around, he hadn't seen that Eldon had come up the stairs after him and was looking on, eyes wide with fear. Behind him looking very angry was Ada. Gwynne ran into Ada's arm sobbing profusely, her clothes and hair dishevelled.

"Eldon, call an ambulance for Mr. Jones, please," Ada said calmly turning to Eldon, who shot to it. Ivor was beginning to come around slightly and was moaning.

"We all saw it," said Ada to everyone in tones of authority. "Ivor pulled the first punch – then slipped and fell!"

Eldon and Gwynne nodded meekly in agreement.

The rest was a bit of a blur. Ada sat Gwynne down, and tidied her blouse and hair.

She ordered Eldon to make her a hot drink.

"You're to go home, have the rest of the day off sick, I'll see you get paid." Ada said to Gwynne.

Next Ada turned to Evan.

"Bloody bastard!" She spat. "That's not the first time he's tried it with young office girls, no wonder they don't last here. Come on I'll see you off the premises."

She took Evan's arm and escorted him down the stairs. "I'll see you get paid for all of today, and give you a reference if you need one, make sure it comes directly to me for my attention. Can't do much about your job though, sorry."

Evan had come to respect Ada a lot. "What will you do?" He asked her. "Probably time to get another job I think, mind you he'll be laid up for some while." She winked.

Evan turned to take her hand, he suddenly had the most brilliant thought, he had the Land Rover and he was well liked at the farms and stables he delivered to.

"Tell you what" he said. "Can you supply me a list of all your clients?"

"Sure," she said. "I can take a photocopy for you, I'll make sure I post it today."

"What are you going to do?" She asked curiously.

"Well, I have my Land Rover sitting there, I'm going to offer my services as supplier to some of your businesses!"

"Good for you," she said with a chuckle. "Hey, Eldon!" She called up the stairs, "get that load of feed off the van into Evan's Land Rover sharpish, will you!"

Evan looked at her and smiled.

"Well, there are load of clients needing their supplies today, and no-one else to do it. Eldon's not passed his test yet, and I'm not doing it. I'll take the amount for the feed out of your wages – you'll get a big discount of course!" She winked again. "Helping us out of trouble at the last minute like that! Go on get loading, the ambulance will be blocking up the yard soon."

Evan did what he was bid, he had a quiet word with Eldon, the youth was still shaking from what he had witnessed.

"Get another job, Ada will give you a reference, I know it's hard, but it's just not worth it here." The youth nodded, he was too shaken to speak. He was a quiet, well behaved lad from a good gospel fearing home.

Ada was as good as her word. The next day a list of suppliers and clients arrived at the bakery for Evan. The first week he was able to pick up the rest of the feedstuffs from the yard, after that he was on his own. He secured Owain's barn and the feedstuffs were stored there. He was not going to take on the whole area, just the parts nearer Brynafon. It would see him by, and his clients seemed unphased that their supplier had changed, Evan was the same delivery driver they had got to know and like, and above all he was reliable. He heard later that Ivor returned to work three months later, minus any staff. He had had to drive the van himself, on the first incline to the river the brakes on the van had completed failed and Ivor had crashed heavily into the stone wall, another three-month spell in hospital followed.

"I'm so proud of you!" Said Ruby, when he had broken the news to her at the end of that first tumultuous day. "You saved that poor girl, she needed a hero like you!"

In all it fitted in a lot better with Evan's plans for a hill farm, and he remembered, after all, all his life he had been very lucky.

Chapter 22

Ruby received good news that Monday, she had had an article published in "Antiquities" about The Hill. It was a couple of sides with photographs, diagrams and Ruby's drawings. Ruby was extremely pleased, it was hard as an unknown to get published, and this boded well for her Masters. The article was photocopied and put on the wall of the café proudly. Christian, the museum curator, wrote a card to congratulate her having just read it in his subscription to the magazine. He also had news of a Roman dig in the New Town, a Roman fort settlement or Vica had been found in meadows south of New Town, it was on a greenfield site near the railway where a new supermarket was due to go up. They were looking for diggers, he was going to get a sabbatical to dig, did she want to apply too? Ruby definitely did! If Evan had any doubts about Ruby and Christian working together, he was wise enough to keep it quiet. It was true, Christian had shown no interest in her other than professional, and vice versa with Ruby. Besides a lot of people would be involved in the dig, and Ruby would be coming home every night. He couldn't keep her cocooned up in Brynafon for ever.

Someone else less welcome had come to the New Town too. He sat there broodily in the pub barely sipping his whisky. He had followed the trail this far, but now it had gone cold. It was a Friday night, the seedy pub at the lower end of the New Town was half full.

He had taken off his motorcycle jacket and it was laid on the chair beside him. Someone somewhere must know something? Thought Ruby's father. He knew now she had definitely travelled by bus to the New Town, but what after that? He could not believe his daughter had been so clever to elude him so far. He had been tantalising close to her a few times, but each time she had eluded him, even when he shot at her in car park at Chester.

Two lads came over and sat on the thread bare and dirty chairs opposite him. They were the usual underachievers he thought, not very bright, drank too much and were parochial. They both had strong local accents, they were talking about the football game this weekend in the New Town, their team was losing badly. They talked about girls for a bit, one appeared to have a long-suffering girlfriend. Ruby's father was damned fed up, he was sitting here on a Friday next to these two-low life's all because of his bloody daughter, Ruby. Why couldn't she just do what she was told? Why couldn't she just submit to him?

"I've got to get back to Brynafon now, mate." One of the lads was saying, "Mum creates if I'm late for supper, stupid woman!"

So, at least one of these guys was from Brynafon, he'd drawn a blank there last time, but what was there to lose? He would try again.

"Excuse me," he said turning to them. "One of you two guys are from Brynafon?"

The thicker built, obvious leader of the two turned stare at him.

"We're both from there, only I chose to get out of that dump. What of it, what's it to you?"

The guy sounded belligerent. Ruby's father had overheard he was called Gareth. The same Gareth that Evan had decked all those years before in the school playground. He still held a long-time grudge against Evan for that.

"Well, there's another drink in it for both of you, if you can just answer a few questions for me?" Ruby's father was all charm.

Gareth snorted: "Make that a double brandy then, the same for my mate here." Gareth burped an intoxicated breath full of beer. The slighter guy sat down again.

"Don't mind if I do." He said. He was called Mick, Evan's former friend who had been so rude to Ruby in the Dragon and Dagger, and who Evan had also decked. Mick's life had deteriorated in many ways since he had fallen out with Evan, and he had never had the decency or manliness to front up to Ruby or Evan and apologise to them. Gareth was his one and only so-called mate now. He looked up to, and kept in with Gareth at all costs.

Ruby's father fetched the drinks, all smiles. "Kind of you to help me out fellers." He said on his return. He put the drinks down, carefully avoiding the couple of patches of chewing gum stuck to the table. The lads did not notice he had not bought a drink for himself, they busily guzzled into the drinks greedily. Mick coughed and spluttered, he'd never tasted brandy before and had tried to guzzle it like he had his beer. Ruby's Dad inwardly grimaced at their uncouthness.

He produced the now well-worn photograph of Ruby in her school hat.

"Have you seen this girl, or know of her where a bouts, she's a runaway and her parents are very anxious to make sure she is safe."

These two were cheap with their information, he thought.

Gareth squinted at the photo. "What do yer think?" he said. "Might be her?" The other guy nodded, "and if we do know her, we expect a reward for the information – a large one!" Said Gareth with a smirk. He was enjoying himself. He puffed himself up importantly.

"Oh, of course," said Ruby's father, with an encouraging smile. "There will be, a large one, her parents are really rather well off, and will pay well for a positive outcome, I can assure you."

Gareth seemed satisfied with his.

"Yeah, well I think it's this girl called Red, local Brynafon whore, she came in January, was sleeping at the bus shelter, then she hitched up with Evan Davies, local estate agent."

If Ruby's father was shocked at his daughter being called the local whore, he didn't show it, he didn't blink an eye lid.

"Is she still there?" He asked.

"Expect so." Said Gareth. Gareth hadn't heard Ruby had married Evan, he never went back to Brynafon to see his mum.

"And where does she live?" He asked, getting information from these two was like getting blood out of a stone he thought.

"Evan's a right wack job, mental, hears the rocks singing," Gareth made the appropriate looney hand gestures.

"He's got this shepherd's hut up on The Hill in Brynafon where he lives, guess you could try there." Said Mick helpfully. He took a sip of the brandy this time, but still spluttered.

"Thank you, gentleman, a pleasure doing business with you" said Ruby's Dad. He handed out a £100 to them each, their eyes widened, "I'll just give the parents the news now, and if I can take your addresses, I'll send you a cheque for the reward money when I find her." He quickly appeared to jot down their addresses, then he whipped out his mobile phone and stood up, standing some distance away as if to get a signal.

The thin youth, Mick, was the first to go, he lurched out unsteadily and into the carpark. It was a rainy night which helped Ruby's Dad's intention, there were not many people on the streets. Mick lurched unsteadily to his car, a beaten-up Ford Fiesta, fumbled for his keys in his pocket – and knew no more. The blow to his neck broke it cleanly, he was swiftly dragged underneath a nearby parked transit van, which on leaving drove over his body.

Ruby's Dad slipped quietly back into the bar, he ordered another drink, which he didn't drink. He only had to wait for five minutes before Gareth, belching, lurched towards the gents. Ruby's Dad quietly and swiftly followed him in. Gareth never came out, he was found five minutes later with his skull severely fractured, he had clearly fallen hard on the urinals in his drunken state, the autopsy was to prove he was double over the limit for driving. No one had seen anything and the CCTV cameras had not worked for some time, any way a rat seemed to have frayed the cables.

Chapter 23

The small film crew that came to Brynafon was also unexpected. They had come from Cardiff and had been told to make a film about off the beaten track unknown and unspoilt gems of villages in South Wales. They had a week to film, time was tight and money was even tighter, and the weather had not been kind to them, for three days it had rained constantly and filming was impossible. It was the young director's first big assignment, and he was eager to make it work. He's filmed three good places so far, he hoped to make Brynafon his fourth. He heard about it quite by chance, he'd seen an article in a local magazine about a revamped bakery selling its own artisan bread and café in the "sleepy, pretty village of Brynafon." He and the rest of his crew had never heard of the place, but it was worth giving it a shot. This could be just the one he was looking for, and it was off the beaten track, that was for sure.

His team arrived late the same evening as Ruby's father had visited the pub in the New Town. The young director had decided to make an early start tomorrow with his team, and he was in luck, there was room for him and his crew at the one pub in Brynafon, the Dragon and Dagger, funny name, he thought.

He looked at the internet sources for Brynafon as his crew headed their vehicle through the New Town, gosh the New Town looked an uninspiring industrial ghetto, the heavy rain now coming down made it even more dreary, he thought, he just hoped Brynafon was as good as the magazine writer had made out. Their car began to climb steeply up to Brynafon, it was absolutely pouring now, a real Autumn gale, the first one of the season, water poured down on to the side of the road from above, together with a small cascade of rocks and earth, gosh he would be glad to get there safely. Fortunately, the storm was due to blow through by tomorrow. He found out that there was a place called The Hill in Brynafon and that Saxon finds had recently been discovered there, well that was interesting he thought. The finds were exhibited in a museum in the New Town he had just driven through, he scrolled further. The Victorian pub they were staying at was named after a Saxon dagger that had been found when the pub was constructed. Brynafon was becoming a popular place for walkers and cyclist, and there was a new horse trekking centre too, promising, he thought. He found a photograph of the bakery café, it looked pretty he thought, kind of oldie worldie, with its bunting and flower planted mangers, and it looked over a rather quaint little market square with a horse trough, pump and memorial cross. There was only the one recent photo of the town, in the online edition of the Welcome Wales magazine. It showed the pub, a rather severe looking chapel, a school and two rows of terraced houses with brightly painted front doors and pretty gardens. He only hoped there were still some flowers left after this storm.

They arrived in the full force of the gale; the wind tore at the car doors as they opened them. They were drenched within seconds. They decided to leave the film gear in the car, the landlord said it would be perfectly safe there. The young director looked over towards the bakery through the rain and the gloom, yes it looked pretty enough, with the sun shining it would look very pretty indeed.

They had just thankfully embarked inside the pub, where the landlord and landlady were cheery and friendly, and a welcoming roaring fire was going full blast, when a motorbike roared into the village. It was an old Enfield, the rider asked a drinker coming out of the pub where The Hill was. The farmer pointed to behind Owain's farm house.

"Behind there," he said, hurrying to his Land Rover. Why on earth some guy was asking him where The Hill was in weather like this was beyond him, but some tourists had funny ideas, and absolutely no sense, and this guy definitely wasn't local, the accent was far too English and plummy. They ought to try being out in all weathers with their flocks some time like he was, he thought. The rain was coming down in torrents, the farmer did not look behind him, he could scarcely see in front of him, the rain was overwhelming his wiper blades. There was a crack and lightening blazed across the sky. Why the hell had he gone for a drink on a night like this? He'd been caught out. At least with the lightening he could see the road ahead of him now, as he pulled out. He didn't see the motorcyclist make his way over the road to Owain's farm, and tentatively find his way to a rusty gate at the rear of the building. The motorcyclist stopped for a minute getting his bearings, he took off his crash helmet. The lightening flashed and the thunder roared deafeningly, echoing all around the hills. One clap of thunder rolling into the next. The motorcyclist glanced up, where was it this shepherd's hut? Surely, he wouldn't have to climb up The Hill in weather like this? What did they mean a hill, it was more of a blob, still it would give him a good view of the surrounding area. The rain was lashing down now, he could hardly see a metre in front of him. He orientated himself on the Hill, and started to climb up. His leathers were soaked already and his motorbike boots were slick with mud and beginning to leak. Slipping and sliding it took him a good few minutes to climb to the top of The Hill. There were no lights on in any of the terrace windows, he wondered whether the power had now gone out. Good, that was a bonus.

He stood erect on The Hill despite the wind tearing at him, he surveyed all around him, there it was, the little shepherd's hut in dark green, with no lights on it blended well into the side of The Hill. No lights were good news for him, if Ruby was there, she was sleeping unawares. He was unaware that Ruby and Evan were blissfully asleep in their new bakery accommodation.

He stood like a glistening black raven, a harbinger of doom, triumphant, proud, he would have his revenge on his unyielding daughter. The lightening brought him in to sharp relief against The Hill, he felt invincible, powerful, almighty. His penis rose in his trousers.

Suddenly, the ground beneath his feet gave way and he was falling, falling, sucked into a dark hellish abyss.

Evan was up early to check the sheep, it had been a dreadful storm, but he and Ruby had slept cosily enough, power had just been restored in the last five minutes so Evan could gratefully have a cup of tea. He pulled on his wellies, it would be very wet and slippery underfoot. He did the rounds of the barns first, one of the tin roofs had half peeled back, he would have to fix that, but fortunately the sheep that were in there had huddled against the wall.

The chickens were fine too, their coop had been overturned by the wind, they were a bit indignant when he carefully righted it, but they were all OK too. Next, he made for The Hill, at first, he glanced at the sheep, grazing down by the hedge line, they looked a bit higher up than normal - peculiar. but as he looked up, he at first could not take it in.....The Hill was.... gone! There was just a large gaping hole where it had been, a pile of mud and debris had ended up by the hedge line, and that's what the sheep were standing on. He stood there open mouthed, gaping, then he ran up as fast as he could, not thinking about this safety.

Cautiously he peered over the edge of the hole.....

There lying some 12 feet below him were two skeletons, clearly a man and a woman. They lay side by side on a slab bed. He had a shield boss over his belly, and the remains of a spear in one hand, in his other hand he had a golden sword, on where his waist would have been was a bronze buckle. The woman had a gold head band, an intricate necklace around what would have been her neck, and she had a gold brooch on her shoulder blade, around where her waist would have been was a gold medallion belt.

Evan gasped audibly, he couldn't believe his eyes. There were more things as well, a pile of coins and other gold items, that had originally been in a chest. The cavity had other items in it too.

There were drinking vessels, gold plates, ironwork and a stone quern stone. Evan gaped, but there was something else as well, on the floor having just missed the lying female skeleton was a man in black motorcycle leathers! The grotesque angle of his head on his neck told Evan that his neck was broken. The man lay on his back, his face was white, but Evan was sure of his identity....

This was Ruby's father!

He had suffered the same broken neck as he had meted out just a few hours before to the young man in the New Town pub car park.

Evan stood there, perfectly still, just surveying the scene for a good five minutes, then he turned and ran to get Ruby.

He wasn't sure how Ruby would react, it was a truly wondrous find, a complete Saxon burial chamber – but in the middle of it laid her father.

He took Ruby up to The Hill hand in hand.

"My God!" Exclaimed Ruby. She too stood motionless and mouth gaping. "A Saxon burial – how amazing, that mound of coins and is clearly where the finds were coming from, and look the lady has lost her left and hand, and probably the ring, my ring that was on it...... oh!"

Ruby stopped short, like Evan she had just seen the black leather clad biker lying dead in the shadow of the slate bed in the burial chamber.

"Is that – is that my father?" She asked Evan.

"I think so, who else could it be?" Said Evan putting his arms around her shoulders. He knew he should have felt some remorse about the death of this man, but he didn't. He just felt relief, colossal relief, now he and Ruby could live a normal life without fear. His worst nightmare lay there dead in the tomb.

Ruby peered over the edge, she seemed unperturbed. "It's certainly the right height, and weight, but we won't know definitely. But it must be, who else would be insane enough to be wandering a hillside in motorbike gear in a storm like last night? Here, Evan can you fetch me a ladder and a rope? I need to know for certain. You better ring the police and Dr. Forster, she'll want to see the burial chamber immediately!"

Dr. Forster was staying with Jed at Manor Farm for a few days before starting lecturing again, as he had promised she would. Evan did as he was told swiftly, he still felt a bit numb, and some of that he had to admit because his beloved Hill was no more, it had revealed its secrets at long last, and it seemed almost by divine retribution, had destroyed Ruby's Father in so doing. It seemed to Evan that his Hill had protected and looked after them, he had worked over it all these years, and now it had had repaid him. It had done the ultimate in protecting them – by killing Ruby's mad, bad, Dad.

Evan came swiftly back with the ladder, both Dr. Forster and the police and a fire crew were on their way.

"Are you sure it's safe?" Asked Evan, as Ruby tied to a line descended the ladder.

"That's why I've got the rope, if there is a problem you can haul me up quickly!"

Evan nodded. Ruby was down in an instant, she carefully looked around her at the burial chamber.

"It's amazing!" She said. "All the gold has been washed clean by the storm, it's just as good as the Sutton Hoo site or that of Prittlewell Priory! In fact, it's remarkable similar to the Prittlewell Priory site." She bent down, and grimly peered at the biker. White hair, and dull open fish like eyes stared unseeingly up at her. "It's him alright." She said matter of factly. "Thank God for that!" Ruby wasn't fazed by a dead body, even her own father's, she had seen plenty of skeletal dead bodies before in her digs. Never the less she said a quick prayer for the dead of her father, one she had learnt at the convent school.

"Eternal rest grant unto him, O Lord, may his soul rest in peace, Amen!" She made the sign of the cross and hurriedly climbed back up the ladder.

Ruby and Evan just stood there hand in hand looking in. It felt to Evan that Ruby's Father was desecrating a grave, and he would be glad when his body had been removed from the site.

Dr Forster was the first to arrive. She hurried up slope.

"Goodness! How remarkable, extraordinary! To have a Saxon burial chamber this far West is extraordinary! See Evan, look the couple, probably husband and wife are buried in a type of room or small hall with all the things they would need for their after life! Over there is a cooking pot, and there are even some dice or something like that for them to play with! And…. good God! Who's that and what's he doing down there!"

"My Father!" Said Ruby.

"Goodness!" Said Dr. Forster again.

"I only imagine he thought I was in the shepherd's hut and as he came to get me The Hill caved in!" Remarked Ruby.

"I'm sure the Saxons would say that their gods had had their vengeance on him!" Said Dr. Forster vehemently. She stared again. "I procured the money for the dig, so now this'll just be an excavation!"

This time Evan had no objections.

It was some thirty minutes later that the police the fire crew arrived. The police took a statement. Who had found the body?

"I did," said Evan.

Who owned the land? Evan said he did, they took his name and contact details.

Did they know the deceased?

"Yes" Ruby said it was her Father, she gave his name, Captain Rupert Hetherington-Whyte. Had anyone been down there? Ruby said she had, she wanted to check if he was still alive. Did they know when the collapse had occurred? No, just sometime last night, and were the other skeletons definitely old? Dr. Forster introduced herself and verified they were Saxon. Later an officer would remove an Enfield motorbike from the car park of the Dragon and Dagger.

There was never any connection made with the two lads who had died at the seedy New Town pub, which closed bankrupt later that week. It was thought that both deaths were unfortunate coincidences, the young man in the car park having slipped and broken his neck in a fall in the wet while intoxicated, slipping under a vehicle which had then run over him.

The other had just slipped in the dirty urinals, where the wet state of the floor due to a leak in the urinals, had contributed to him banging the back of his head and dying. It was very unusual, but not seen as suspicious in anyway, drinkers vaguely remembered the two young men, but couldn't remember anyone else, and were not helpful or forthcoming with information, they didn't want to know. It was that type of place.

The fire brigade efficiently extracted Ruby's Father's body from his tomb in the burial chamber. The only odd thing about the corpse was that he was carrying a pistol and a sheath knife. Ruby just shrugged. He was in some sort of special intelligence army unit, she said. That was all she knew.

It was at that point the film crew arrived. They had heard what had happened from the police enquiries at the pub. They couldn't believe their luck. The young director, who had previously been in news hurriedly organised his team to film the burial chamber. Dr. Forster was adamant the exact whereabouts must be kept a secret, looting of the burial chamber would occur otherwise. The Director agreed in return for permission to film. He asked Evan Dr. Forster and Ruby questions about the site, and of course about the modern dead body that had been deposited in it. Ruby said as little as possible on that score. It was on the Welsh evening news that night, and picked up by the national news and media the next day.

The young director would film the café and village when he had finished the news clip.

Brynafon had already turned up trumps as far as he was concerned, and the bakery, café and village were given a very rosy review later. One of his crew had even clocked Ruby as being "Red" from the band Rainbow Revivals, he had been at the Cardiff festival concert.

After the crew had filmed the burial chamber, Ruby, Evan and Dr. Forster covered the chamber with tarpaulins weighed down by rocks to keep the site dry. Evan also put up electric fencing, he didn't want any sheep or a walker falling in. The police had erected a cordon round it with no entry and danger signs, the Hill became quiet again as the sheep munched around it.

Chapter 24

One thing was missing from the scene at The Hill burial chamber, and Evan suddenly realised it was Owain, come to think of it he had not seen him or Meg all morning. It wasn't like him not to be up and about early attending to his sheep. Evan excused himself, whispering "Owain" to Ruby as he rushed down the slope to the farmhouse. Something must be wrong with him.

He called Owain's name loudly as he entered the farm house via the back door as always. All was quiet, the curtains were still closed. He drew them, should he look in the bedroom or sitting room first? He hesitated a second then rushed into the sitting room, he switched on the light. Owain was in his high-backed chair, his head slumped forward.

"Owain!" He shouted. Meg was at Owain's feet her face doleful and her head down on her crossed paws, just waiting patiently for her master to respond. Evan took Owain's shoulder and shook it gently. Still nothing, Evan quickly opened the curtains to get more light in. He turned around to face Owain, Owain was grey, there was no breath, no heartbeat. Evan quickly pulled Owain on to the floor to resuscitate him, but as he did so he realised Owain was cold, this time he would not be able

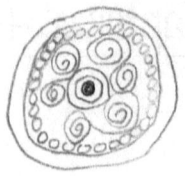

Ruby's drawing of Saxon brooch

Ruby's drawing of a Saxon coin from Mercia

Ruby's drawing of a Saxon ruby ring

to resuscitate him. Evan stood there, tears welling up in his eyes and then streaming down his face, as he cried quietly. Owain was dead.

He suddenly noticed a letter in an envelope that had fallen from Owain's lap on to the floor. He picked it up, it had his name on it. Swiftly he opened it, it was written in Welsh in Owain's copper plate hand and read:

"Evan, don't be sad for me boy when you read this. Take Meg and look after her for me, that's all I ask, she trusts you.

I've known for some time I've got heart problems, got it confirmed at the hospital. It wasn't going to get better. I didn't want any "treatment", don't want to end my last days in hospital away from Meg and my farm and my sheep. I knew my time was soon, same as the sheep seem to know.

See if I can be buried on The Hill will you boy? If there has to be a service the Pastor can do it. There's money in the black mug in the kitchen cupboard to cover the cost.

I have always thought of you as the son I never had, and I have left the farm and house to you. I know you will take care of the sheep, and who knows with a pair of strong young arms it might thrive and prosper again? It's all legal, it is written in my will at my solicitors, Thrupp, Jones and Jones.

It's all yours my boy. Now take Meg and go and feed her, get on with you my boy!

God Bless you
Owain."

Evan fetched Meg's lead, she would not want to leave Owain, he fed her, taking with him her food, bowl and old bed.

"Come on Meg," he said quietly to her. "It's up to us now!" As he quietly closed the back door of the farmhouse behind him.

THE END